UALALAPI

ADAMASTOR SERIES
Series Editor: Anna M. Klobucka

Chaos and Splendor & Other Essays
Eduardo Lourenço
Edited by Carlos Veloso

Producing Presences: Branching Out from Gumbrecht's Work
Edited by Victor K. Mendes and João Cezar de Castro Rocha

Sonnets and Other Poems
Luís de Camões
Translated by Richard Zenith

The Traveling Eye: Retrospection, Vision, and Prophecy in the Portuguese Renaissance
Fernando Gil and Helder Macedo
Translated by K. David Jackson, Anna M. Klobucka, Kenneth Krabbenhoft, Richard Zenith

The Sermon of Saint Anthony to the Fish and Other Texts
António Vieira
Introduction by Vincent Barletta
Translated by Gregory Rabassa

The Correspondence of Fradique Mendes: A Novel
José de Maria de Eça de Queirós
Translated by Gregory Rabassa

The Relic: A Novel
José de Maria de Eça de Queirós
Preface by Harold Bloom
Translated by Aubrey F. G. Bell

Maiden and Modest: A Renaissance Pastoral Romance
Bernardim Ribeiro
Foreword by Earl E. Fitz
Translated by Gregory Rabassa

Saint Christopher: A Novella
José de Maria de Eça de Queirós
Foreword by Carlos Reis
Translated by Gregory Rabassa and Earl E. Fitz

Exemplary Tales
Sophia de Mello Breyner Andresen
Introduction by Cláudia Pazos-Alonso
Translated by Alexis Levitin

Ualalapi: Fragments from the End of Empire
Ungulani Ba Ka Khosa
Foreword by Phillip Rothwell
Translated by Richard Bartlett and Isaura de Oliveira

UALALAPI

FRAGMENTS FROM THE END OF EMPIRE

Tagus Press • UMass Dartmouth • Dartmouth, Massachusetts

UNGULANI BA KA KHOSA

Translated from the Portuguese by
Richard Bartlett and Isaura de Oliveira

*Tagus Press is the publishing arm of the
Center for Portuguese Studies and Culture at
the University of Massachusetts Dartmouth.*
Center Director: Victor K. Mendes

Adamastor Series 11
Tagus Press at UMass Dartmouth
www.portstudies.umassd.edu
original Portuguese text © 1987 Ungulani Ba Ka Khosa;
published by arrangement with the author;
translation © 2017 Richard Bartlett and Isaura de Oliveira;
foreword © 2017 Phillip Rothwell

All rights reserved
Manufactured in the United States of America

Series Editor: Anna M. Klobucka
Executive Editor: Mario Pereira
Manuscript Editor: Anna M. Klobucka
Production Editor: Susan Abel
Copyedited by Elizabeth Forsaith
Designed by Mindy Basinger Hill
Typeset in Adobe Caslon Pro

For all inquiries, please contact:
Tagus Press • Center for Portuguese Studies and Culture
UMass Dartmouth • 285 Old Westport Road
North Dartmouth MA 02747–2300
Tel. 508–999–8255 • Fax 508–999–9272
www.portstudies.umassd.edu

Library of Congress Cataloging-in-Publication Data available upon request

Paperback ISBN: 978-1-933227-73-3
Ebook ISBN: 978-1-933227-74-0

5 4 3 2 1

CONTENTS

Foreword Lessons to Power from the Past *Phillip Rothwell* ix

Author's Note xv

Fragments from the End (1) 5

Ualalapi 7

Fragments from the End (2) 23

Mputa's Death 25

Fragments from the End (3) 35

Damboia 37

Fragments from the End (4) 49

A Siege or Fragments of a Siege 51

Fragments from the End (5) 61

Manua's Diary 63

Fragments from the End (6) 75

Ngungunhane's Last Speech 77

FOREWORD
LESSONS TO POWER FROM THE PAST

Phillip Rothwell, University of Oxford

Ungulani Ba Ka Khosa was born in Sofala, in the center of Mozambique, in 1957. He began publishing short stories in local newspapers in 1982, and was involved in the production of the literary journal *Charrua*. The journal, founded in 1984, was the first concerted effort in Mozambique to interrogate the nation's incipient identity and detach it from the legacy of an ideologically loaded poetry of the liberation struggle.

Mozambique gained independence from Portugal in 1975. The nation's independence movement, FRELIMO, took power under the leadership of one of Africa's most charismatic freedom fighters, Samora Machel. His government immediately embarked on an ambitious program to develop the country and to educate formally a largely illiterate, diverse, and rural population. In a country with multiple ethnicities and at least forty languages spoken within its frontiers, FRELIMO opted for Portuguese as the official language of unity through which the Mozambican nation would be imagined.

Ungulani trained as a teacher, with a specialty in history, as part of FRELIMO's education drive. He then began to work for the Mozambican Writers' Association. In 1987, the association published *Ualalapi*. The book was republished the same year by Caminho, one of Portugal's most prestigious presses, which showcases works from Portuguese-speaking Africa. That publishing break brought Ungulani a degree of international prominence as an innovative writer who experimented with form. He drew on Mozambique's colonial history in a way that challenged FRELIMO's narrative of the nation. In 1990, the book won the Grande Prémio da Ficção Narrativa, sharing the prize with *Voices Made Night* by Mozambique's most famous contemporary writer, Mia Couto.

The 1980s in Mozambique was a troubled decade. The initial euphoria and optimism that accompanied independence were dampened by a violent civil conflict, exacerbated by the politics of the Cold War. An increasingly desperate apartheid-era South Africa also lashed out against Mozambique. Faced with economic collapse and political destabilization, the FRELIMO government was unable to deliver its national development agenda, particularly in the more densely populated north of the country.

From its beginnings, the FRELIMO leadership had been perceived as dominated by southerners. Its founding president, Eduardo Mondlane, assassinated before independence, and his successor, Samora Machel, were born in the southern province of Gaza. When Machel died in a suspicious plane crash in 1986, FRELIMO chose another Gazan, Joaquim Alberto Chissano, to replace him. FRELIMO's opponents repeatedly complained about a perceived southern hegemony, equating it to an imperial order.

Machel, a committed Marxist who had led FRELIMO's military fight against the Portuguese, was an inspiring leader, with a clear vision of where he wanted to take Mozambique. However, he was also autocratic and intolerant of opposition. His government clumsily sanctioned a number of measures that replicated the authoritarianism of the colonial regime. For those who were affected, the mandatory "villagization" of rural populations at risk of flooding and scant regard for their traditional belief systems seemed more like a colonial policy of concentration camps than a public health measure. In the 1980s, the infamous "Operation Production" swept up tens of thousands of people deemed to be vagrants in cities predominantly in the South and relocated them to labor camps in the North. The policy bore more than a passing resemblance to the Portuguese practice of forced labor. Single women were a particularly targeted group. Suspected of prostitution, they were often sent to reeducation camps. As FRELIMO haphazardly alienated large sections of the population, it also oversaw the rapid contraction of the Mozambican economy, debilitated by the protracted civil war and a certain degree of fiscal incompetence. By the mid-1980s, Mozambique was enduring a vicious cycle of violence and an increasingly repressive regime, and had plunged down the global poverty league tables.

Against that backdrop, Ungulani wrote *Ualalapi*. He chose the topic of Ngungunhane not only because of his interest in history, but also as a means of critiquing the FRELIMO government. Ngungunhane, around whom the narratives in the collection revolve, was reclaimed by the regime as a national hero. He became a staple of the national curriculum in history. His feats in resisting the Portuguese occupation of the South of Mozambique in the latter part of the nineteenth century were celebrated as a precursor to the twentieth-century struggle for independence. In 1985, an urn supposedly containing his mortal remains was ceremoniously transported back to Mozambique from the Azores, where he died in exile in 1906. In fact, it is highly improbable that the ashes were his, but the ritual was used as part of the celebration of ten years of Mozambican independence, and the parallels between Samora Machel and Ngungunhane abounded.

Ngungunhane was the last ruler of the Gaza Empire. One of the characteristics of Portuguese colonialism in Mozambique until the end of the nineteenth century was the sparse physical presence of Europeans. Though nominally ruled by Portugal, large tracts of Mozambique were the dominions of a range of different fiefdoms. Toward the end of the first quarter of the nineteenth century, a group of disaffected Nguni fleeing drought and the grip of Shaka Zulu invaded the South of Mozambique, conquering and unifying the territory into what became known as the Gaza Empire. When its first emperor, Shoshangane, died in 1858, the stability of his three-decade-long reign was replaced by a succession crisis, in which two half brothers, Muzila and Mawewe, fought long and hard for supremacy. They involved the British and the Portuguese in their intrigues, playing one imperial power off against the other. Eventually, Muzila defeated Mawewe, but not before seven years of warfare had destroyed much of the Gaza Empire.

In 1884, following Muzila's death, his son Mudungazi ascended to the throne by killing his half brother Mafemane. In the oral traditions of the area, that fratricide was encouraged by Muzila's favorite sister, Damboia, a strong-willed woman often depicted as debauched. Mudungazi took the name Ngungunhane, which means "invincible and terrifying" but can also mean "against general expectations," an allusion to the fact that he was not first in line to the throne. His reign lasted until late 1895, when Mouzinho de Albuquerque, the Portuguese military governor of Gaza province, captured him. The case was widely covered at the time by the Portuguese press, particularly when Ngungunhane and members of his entourage were deported to Lisbon and put on display as imperial curios before being exiled to the Azores. In exile, Ngungunhane was given the name Reinaldo Ferreira, baptized, and taught to read.

By most standards, his reign was a disaster. The Gaza Empire came to an end on his watch, as Portugal sought to shore up its effective occupation of Africa following a change in European imperial dynamics. The primacy of the Nguni over southern Mozambique was over. They had used a policy of assimilating the cultures and traditions of those they conquered as a means of gaining the allegiance of the vanquished. Not all of those they had ruled were sorry to see them defeated by the Portuguese. In particular, the Chope, an ethnic group based to the North of Gaza, detested them. The Nguni, notably under Muzila, were especially brutal toward the Chope, a proud nation they considered unassimilable. And yet, FRELIMO appropriated Ngungunhane as a symbol of Mozambican nationalism with roots beyond urban elites educated in Portuguese mores.

In *Ualalapi*, Ungulani challenges that appropriation, portraying a despot, whose prophecies in the book's final chapter, "Ngungunhane's Last Speech," are in the words of Jared Banks, "less a lament for the fate of his fellow Africans than a curse for their having rejected his empire in favor of another" (Banks 2001, 1). The promotion in the 1980s of Ngungunhane to hero status was a highly ideological act that either ignored or deliberately downplayed the violence and tyranny that were markers of the Gaza Empire.

Ungulani takes a fresh look at the history of late nineteenth-century Mozambique and uses it to question the machinations of power in 1980s Mozambique. He draws on multiple historical figures from beyond the Gaza Empire, including António Enes (an interim governor of Mozambique), Ayres d'Ornellas (a military commander involved in the so-called pacification campaigns that helped bring down

Ngungunhane), and George Liengme (a Swiss evangelical who frequented Ngungunhane's court). He fuses their accounts and perspectives with those from the peripheries of Ngungunhane's household. Thus, he gives voice to those whom Mozambique's commemorative and nationalistic history had silenced or overlooked. The result is not a true account of Ngungunhane—as no such thing can exist—but rather a foregrounding of the fragmentary and ideological nature of any attempted historical depiction, and in the process, a thoughtful interrogation of the uses to which those in power put history.

WORKS CONSULTED
AND FURTHER READING

Afolabi, Niyi, ed. *Emerging Perspectives on Ungulani Ba Ka Khosa: Prophet, Trickster and Provocateur.* Trenton, NJ: Africa World Press, 2010.

Banks, Jared. "Adamastorying Mozambique: *Ualalapi* and *Os Lusíadas*." *Luso-Brazilian Review* 37, no. 1 (Summer 2001): 1–16.

FRELIMO. *História de Moçambique.* Porto: Afrontamento, 1971.

Matusse, Gilberto. *A construção da imagem de moçambicanidade em José Craveirinha, Mia Couto e Ungulani Ba Ka Khosa.* Maputo: Universidade Eduardo Mondlane, 1998.

Newitt, Malyn. *A History of Mozambique.* London: Hurst, 1995.

Serra, Carlos, et al. *História de Moçambique,* vol. 1: *Primeiras sociedades sedentárias e impacto dos mercadores* (200/300–1886). Maputo: Universidade Eduardo Mondlane, 1982.

Ungulani Ba Ka Khosa. Interview in *Jornal de Letras, Artes e Ideias,* no. 466 (June 11, 1991): 5–6.

Vilhena, Maria da Conceição. *Gungunhana no seu reino.* Lisbon: Colibri, 1996.

AUTHOR'S NOTE

It is an irrefutable truth that Ngungunhane was emperor of the land of Gaza in the final days of the empire. It is also true that one of the pleasures he cultivated in life was the uncertainty of the actual extent of the lands under his rule. What is in doubt is the fact that Ngungunhane, on the day before his death, arrived at the sad conclusion that the languages of his empire had not created, throughout the empire's existence, the word *emperor*. There are those who say that this lapse was fatal in his life, weakened by long years of exile.

As will be immediately obvious to the reader, throughout this story or stories, the words *emperor*, *king*, and *hosi*—the word in the Tsonga language for king—are used intentionally and anarchically.

UALALAPI

Among those who came was Ngungunhane, whom I recognized immediately, despite never having seen a picture of him at all; he was obviously the chief of a significant race ... He is a tall man ... and although his features are not as outstanding as I had noted in so many of his kind, they are certainly handsome: large forehead, brown and intelligent eyes, and a certain air of grandeur and superiority ...

Ayres d'Ornellas

He was a chronic inebriate. After any of the numerous orgies in which he participated, he looked terrifying with his red eyes, swollen face, and the bestial expression that grew diabolical, horrendous, when in such moments he became enraged ...

Dr. Liengme

I just want to state that I admired the man, who was able to have discussions, over a long period, with clear and logical arguments ...

Ayres d'Ornellas

... but all of his politics was so false, absurd, and full of duplicity that it became difficult to understand his true sentiments.

Dr. Liengme

- Quotes from European figures
- Different perceptions of Ngungunhane
- Came from diaries, reports, excerpts from actual written texts from the period

History is controlled fiction.
Agustina Bessa Luís

FRAGMENTS FROM THE END (1)

Nothing in the world can give the faintest idea of the magnificence of the anthem, the harmony of the song, whose solemn and deep notes, pulsating with enthusiasm from six thousand mouths, made us tremble in our deepest recesses. What majesty, what energy in that music, now considered and slow, almost lifeless, now reborn triumphantly in a wave of passion, in a heated explosion of enthusiasm! And as the groups of warriors marched away, the deep notes still held sway for a long time, echoing off the hills and bush of Manjacaze. Who could the anonymous composer of such beauty be? Whose great soul was able to express the African war in three or four beats, with all the arid crudity of its poetry? Even today my detached ears vibrate with the echo of the terrible Vatua war chant, which so often terrified Chope guards, lost among the thickets of this bush .

Ayres d'Ornellas, "Letters from Africa"

UALALAPI

For Judite Gettessemane

U Ngungunhane! . . .
Uya ngungunya e bafazi ne madoda! . . .
You are Ngungunhane! . . .
You will terrorize women and men! . . .

Anonymous, nineteenth century

I

When they arrived at one of the foothills closest to the village, the warriors sighed with relief on seeing the houses spread out among the trees with centuries-old roots, immersed in a deep silence, typical of that time of day when the sun had majestically passed the halfway point in the cloudless sky, flinging rays that burned the faces, the backs, and the naked chests of the warriors, covered from waist to upper thigh with wild-animal skins.

Ualalapi, at the head of the warriors, looked over the whole village and thought of the *doro,* the name given to the pombe beer prepared in these lands of the Mundau people. He thought of how it would flow down his gullet, with a nice piece of meat, in the shade of a leafy tree, with his wife in front of him stirring up the fire and his son playing, as night was beckoning calmly, bringing with it a waning moon and, in the distance, voices of other men talking into the evening, roaming across the worlds of Nguni bravery from times of war and peace.

He smiled at the warriors accompanying him, laden with fresh meat, the product of a hunt carried out in the interior lands; and he began the descent along a winding path, indifferent to the insistent scratching of the tall bushes that grew on the edges of the path, when, halfway down, he stopped in his tracks, forcing the others to stop and come closer, gathering around him.

Two pangolins, animals of bad omen, shone in the sun in an attitude of complete drowsiness, in the middle of the pathway. Ualalapi looked askance at the warriors who surrounded him and saw the same bright, tremulous, clear, and vacant look in their eyes. He didn't say a word. He touched the fresh meat, a sign of abundance and good fortune, and cast his eyes upon the pangolins, animals of bad omen, as has already been said. And all of them, as if frozen in stone by the inauspicious scene, remained in the same position, feeling the sun beating down on their bodies and the bushes throwing their most daring branches, bent back by contact with the bodies, for several long minutes, until the pangolins recovered their strength and moved off the pathway, leaving it free for the men to pass and for the thoughts they were all thinking to flow.

Ualalapi thought of his son and saw him taking the shield of many battles from against the mud wall. But why his son, he thought, and not the mother of his son, who always offered him her body on moonlit nights and, at times, in moments improper for fornication? He passed his hand over his hair, removing a leaf, looked at the birds flying in silence, and felt a slight shiver over his body. No, it cannot be her, he thought, I left her healthy in body and mind. And as a woman, an Nguni woman, she predicts her own fate. Nor my son, it is impossible, really, how can the child of an Nguni father and mother die unexpectedly at two years of age without ever having been instructed in the use of weapons, as his fathers and grandfathers had been? No, it is impossible, for his family the winds of misfortune cannot arrive just yet. Perhaps for these warriors, he thought, and saw them with heads bowed, as if fearing the earth would open at their feet, tripping over everything and nothing. Not them either, they are commoners, and unhappiness always comes to commoners without omens, since the beginning of time, as obvious as their common lives, without history and destiny except for being born to serve their superiors until their death. To whom could this omen then be directed if I have no relatives besides my wife and son? He looked at the warriors and saw them in the same pensive attitude, thinking of wives and children or of fathers and grandfathers, dispersed throughout the empire without end.

While they thought of this and that, remembering things ancient and present, related to the omens that nature brings without pity to men, they quickened their step in the direction of the nearest village, its alleys deserted, without any sound but the growing rustle of the leaves of the trees and the rising of the dispersed smoke coming from some huts, where the fire obstinately grabbed the logs that were being overwhelmed by the ashes.

They approached the nearest hut and Ualalapi went ahead. A middle-aged woman, seated in front of the house, was breast-feeding a child.

"What's happening, Ma?" asked Ualalapi, squatting and putting his spear down within reach of his right hand.

"The owls were obstinately circling over the houses, screeching all the time and bringing back spirits long asleep that disturbed our minds and provoked some deaths," said the woman with a tired expression, focused on her son, who was randomly moving his feet and eyes, trying to get rid of the flies that kept landing on him.

"Has someone in your family died?"

"My husband."

"I'm sorry, Ma. I'm really very sorry. And the men, where have the men gone?"

"Who has the courage to walk around in these times? They are speaking with their spirits. It was not a man who died, it was an empire."

"Who else died?"

"You will come to know. The chiefs like you are waiting for Mudungazi at the square."

"Okay. How did your husband die?"

"Of fright. But of what importance is an ant compared to an elephant?"

"How often has an ant not killed an elephant, Ma?"

"And how often does the crocodile leave the water, man?"

"Thank you, Ma," said Ualalapi, disturbed. He got up, picked up his spear, and turned to face the warriors who were looking at him, tired of waiting.

"Go put the meat away and wait for further orders. I am going to the square," and he left them without delay, walking quickly, indifferent to the wind that was blowing grains of sand and scattered leaves on the ground, forming small whirlwinds that rose in disorganized circles, again and again touching Ualalapi's body, covered with a layer of blood and the residue of leaves. The leaves were being loosened from his body by the force of the wind, which carried a strange smell, felt in this area in time immemorial when men of other tribes saw their houses collapse from the force of the wind and the rain that covered the land and the bush with muddy and foul-smelling water just as they were finishing the burial of a king of Manica who, as foretold by his *swikiro*—the name given to the Shona mediums—did not have any time to rule other than the number of days equal to the number of fingers he had on his hands. But it was time enough for him to thrive on the sumptuous meals that ended on the fatal day on which he died of congestion.

And Ualalapi, on his way to the square, was now passing the place where the body of the king was laid down, inside a hut, under the attentive gaze of the elite of the kingdom, who had the duty of watching over the putrefaction of the body so that the evil spirits did not take possession of its parts, for days and nights bearing the insupportable smell of the putrid flesh, whose liquids were falling into vessels prepared for that purpose. Ualalapi put his right hand to his nose and went into the square. He looked at the sky and saw the dark and heavy clouds coming down from the heights. The wind whipped the tall and short trees. He approached Mputa, a warrior who would die in a stupid and innocent way but whose face would remain in everyone's memory, as stated by those who predicted his destiny, albeit without specifying the reasons for his death, because in history in which kings and queens participate everyone moves on, even the swikiros who foresee everything.

"What's happening, Mputa?"

"Muzila died."

"How?"

"It has been said that he died of an illness, because for several nights he didn't take his eyes off the ceiling of his house."

"An inhuman death for an Nguni."

"It has been said that his father died in the same way."

"It wasn't their wish, Mputa."

"I know of few kings who died in battle."

"But everyone says that is the best way to die."

"When they address warriors."

"You think too fast."

"That's what war teaches, Ualalapi."

"You're right... Can you smell that stench?"

"It's the smell of death. When a king dies, some of his subjects must accompany him."

"I spoke with a woman who lost her husband."

"There have been other deaths. Old Salama, when she knew of the king's death, went to one of the river's banks and waited for the crocodile incarnations of her ancestors, who came to fetch her after she had been sitting there for half an hour contemplating the waters of the river. Old Lucere died during the siesta, devoured by giant ants that did not leave a piece of flesh on his old body. Chichuaio, entering his house, saw himself surrounded by snakes that fought for possession of his body. And there are further cases, it is always so."

"I know, but it's incredible... How long have you been waiting for Mudungazi?"

"Since the beginning of the afternoon. This smell is bothering me..."

"It is from those long since dead, Mputa."

"Bones don't smell, Ualalapi."

"But the spirits are capable of anything."

"You're right. Let's stand up. Mudungazi is going to show up. How was the hunt?"

"Good. There is lots of meat."

"Abundance in the midst of misfortune."

"That's it," said Ualalapi, cleaning his body. The clouds that were threatening the village began to disperse, carrying the wind and the smell of death that hovered over the village during the week in which Ualalapi was in the interior of the lands of Manica.

II

In a sobbing voice, tearful, but which would gain strength during the course of his speech, as is common with those who have the gift of speaking to the people, Mudungazi began to address the chiefs of the warriors by asserting that the things of the plain have no ending.

We arrived here many, many harvests ago with our spears soaked in blood and our shields tired of protecting us.

We won battles. We opened roads. We planted maize in stony, barren lands. We brought rain to these scorched lands, and we educated people brutalized by the most primitive customs. And today these people are among us, Nguni!

This empire without measure was built by my grandfather after innumerable battles in which he always triumphed. In this empire he spread order, and new customs that we brought. And on his deathbed he indicated his son Muzila, my father, as his successor. Muzila had a man's heart. He was kind. And many took advantage of his kindness. Among them Mawewe, his brother, who by means of a shameful cabal attempted and was able to usurp power without the approval of the spirits and the elite of the kingdom, who had accepted Muzila as the successor because he had been the first to open the grave where his father would rest forever and ever. But Mawewe forgot this and took the throne for a time that history will not record, and if it is recorded, it will be with the treachery engraved on the face of this man whom I do not dare call uncle.

At that time, my warriors, innocent corpses covered the land, and the waters took on the color of blood for weeks on end, forcing people to drink the blood of their dead brothers because they could not stand the thirst that tormented them. And all of this caused by the stubbornness of Mawewe, who insisted on keeping power.

Muzila died, my warriors. At the edge of death he appointed me as his successor. His grave must be opened by me. Do you think history is going to repeat itself?

The warriors, in a precise movement, beat their shields of skin on the ground and said no.

You are with me, said Mudungazi, not because of the loyalty you owe me but because you respect my words. I was expecting this of you.

He stopped his speech for a few moments and ran his gaze with bloodshot eyes over the warriors, who kept silent. The sun was falling. The wind was quiet. White clouds laid themselves upon the dark clouds in the blue sky.

My brother Mafemane, he proceeded, lives only ten miles from here. I believe that he is getting ready to leave with the purpose of opening my father's grave. History must not be repeated. The power belongs to me. Nobody, but nobody can take it from me until my death. The spirits alight on me and keep me company, guiding my lucid and just actions. And I will not allow the same slaughter to happen as at the time of Muzila's enthronement, because I will take action now. The men who do not know me will come to know me. I will not share power. It belongs to me from the day I was born from the womb of Lozia, my mother, Muzila's favorite wife. And I will be feared by everyone because I will not be called Mudungazi but Ngungunhane, much like those deep caves where we throw those condemned to death! The fear and terror of my empire will endure for centuries and centuries and will be known in lands you've never dreamed of! For that reason, my warriors, sharpen your spears. We have to clean, as urgently as possible, the path by which we travel, so that we are not tripped up by possible obstacles.

Thus Mudungazi ended his contact with the warriors. The night came. Followed by his aunt, who went by the name of Damboia,

Mudungazi went to the large hut, swaying his ample flesh, which would not change much until his death in unknown waters, covered in clothes he had always rejected and in the midst of people the color of a skinned goat, who had been very surprised to see a nigger.

III

"You have the habit of climbing the tree by its branches, Mudungazi."
"They understood, Damboia."
"I doubt it."
"For a warrior, just point him at the target."
"And why didn't you name the man who must execute him?"
"I will do it at the break of day. And don't worry about Mafemane: the vultures are already preparing to devour him. Let's drink doro beer to my rise to power over this empire."
"To you, Ngungunhane."
"That's it, Ngungunhane. I'll be forever Ngungunhane and I will die of old age. That's what the spirits wanted."

"What's wrong, Ualalapi?"
"Muzila died."
"I know. But what did Mudungazi say?"
"Mafemane must die."
"Why?"
"Through the door of a house only one can enter at a time."
"And the other must wait in the yard."
"Ah ... Men always avoid turning their backs on someone. It's dangerous."
"Not always. But who is going to kill him?"
"You worry too much. Forget it. Is the water for my bath ready?"

"It's on the fire. This situation bothers me."
"Why?"
"I had strange dreams."
"That's normal in days of mourning."
"I dreamed of your death."
"My death?"
"Yes."
"And how did I die in your dream?"
"You died walking. Your voice supported your lifeless body. I and your son drowned in tears that did not stop falling from our eyes."
"Incredible, but none of this is going to happen, woman."
"I'm scared, Ualalapi. I'm scared. I see lots of blood, blood that flows from our grandparents who came into these lands, killing, and their children and grandchildren remain here, also killing. Blood, Ualalapi, blood! We live on the blood of these innocents. Why, Ualalapi?"
"It's necessary, woman. We are the people chosen by the spirits to spread order in these lands. And it is because of this that we go from victory to victory. And before the green blossoms, it is necessary that the blood water the land. And right now you don't have to worry about anything, because we are in times of peace and mourning."

"And your brothers, Mudungazi?"
"Which ones? Como. Como, Anhane, Mafabaze?"
"Yes."
"They will not have the courage to oppose my orders. The danger is Mafemane. He is the one who must die."

"If you are chosen to kill Mafemane, don't accept, Ualalapi."
"Perhaps I will not be the person chosen. But why?"
"I'm afraid for your life, Ualalapi."

"Don't worry. I will only die in battle like my father who, with four spears embedded in his chest, had the extraordinary courage to throw his spear, which I use today, into the chest of a Tsonga from ten yards away. I will only die in battle, woman. It's my destiny, it is the destiny of all the great Nguni warriors."

"Don't fool yourself, Ualalapi. Many were the warriors who died in a stupid way and without being in battle. Sereko, who killed so many people in battle, died from a snakebite sent by his displeased grandfather. Makuko died in the bush, defecating without pause for fifteen consecutive days. And when he was found, already dead, the shit was still flowing from his body. They had to bury him with the shit that wouldn't stop coming. And you can't run away from this. It is also possible to die outside of battle. And I'm scared, Ualalapi."

"It's a dream, woman."

"And how many times have I been mistaken in my dreams?"

"You may be right, but if I have to die, how can I run away from destiny?"

"Don't say that. You're exasperating. I'm just asking you to refuse the order to kill Mafemane."

"I owe allegiance to Mudungazi."

IV

The sun had not yet burned off the dew when Manhune and the warriors under his command approached Mafemane's village, straining to listen for signs of departure. But the silence, the same silence that was affecting everyone in those days of mourning, covered the huts of Mafemane and his men and women. In the alleys nothing could be seen besides little leaves and pieces of broken pitchers, scattered on the ground. Manhune left most of the warriors accompanying him and took two to the house of Mafemane, which rose in the middle of the village. Something about that silence frightened them because, as they walked to the center of the village, they couldn't hear any noises other than the sound of their bare feet treading on the damp earth. Mafemane, tall, imperturbable, stood in front of his house, arms crossed over his large and strong chest.

"I was waiting for you," said Mafemane, approaching Manhune. "I know that Muzila died. I also know that my brother was chosen as his successor despite me being the first son of Muzila's *inkosikazi,* Fussi. The throne belongs to Mudungazi. I also know that you came with orders to kill me. I am prepared to die. But I ask you to let me say good-bye to my wives and children. Come back at the end of the day."

The words, as if coming from the heights, entered the minds of Manhune and the warriors with such clarity that they were turned to stone by Mafemane's calmness and serenity. Mafemane smiled and glared at them. His eyes were translucent, shining, shocking. Unable to answer, Mudungazi's men began to retreat, their eyes fixed on Mafemane. Manhune tripped, fell, got up, turned his back on Mafemane, and began to walk so fast that the warriors who were waiting for him were surprised and disturbed.

"What's happening, Manhune?"

"Don't ask me anything. Go, let's go to our village."

And he led the way. On arriving at the village, they tried to explain to Mudungazi what they had seen and heard, but Damboia, her eyes sparkling, interposed herself, insulting them as no one had done since the times when they were learning how to use weapons. And to them the reproach seemed unacceptable because it was coming from the mouth of a woman, and a woman of bad reputation, despite her being of royal blood.

"And this is the elite guard you are relying on, Mudungazi? A bunch of cowards, dogs that only know how to bark. What allegiance have you sworn to Mudungazi? What allegiance, you dogs? No, don't answer me, you don't have the right to speak. You should be thrown to the vultures. That's what you deserve, misbegotten brats! You come here trying to convince us that Mafemane, knowing of his death, wanted to say good-bye to his wives and children. Why didn't he do this before? Ah, you dogs, imbeciles, idiots, senseless brats! Mafemane is getting ready to run, and has probably left already. Idiots. And you, Mudungazi, you still have the courage to give shelter to dogs that only know how to bark? If I were you, I would kill them. Let's not waste any more time with these idiots. Go, Maguiguane, Mputa, and Ualalapi. And take the warriors you want. But don't show up in this village without the body of Mafemane, even if you have to make the forest around you disappear. Get going!"

Ualalapi's wife followed her husband with her eyes until he disappeared in the forest. She picked up her son and began to weep. She entered the hut and never left until the death of her son and herself, drowned by tears that did not stop flowing from her staring eyes for eleven days and eleven nights.

Ualalapi, far away from the torment of his wife, approached Mafemane's village. The sun took on a red color. The afternoon was slipping away. When Mafemane's house came into view, Ualalapi stopped with his warriors fifteen yards away. Maguiguane and Mputa went ahead, to the right and left respectively, leaving a corridor in the middle, at the end of which stood Mafemane, with a smile on his lips, waiting for them in front of the doorway.

"I didn't think you'd come," said Mafemane, running his eyes down them, with a penetrating, incisive gaze. "So many people weren't necessary, two would be enough. But I'm ready. You can kill me. I know that you can't go back to your village without my body. I have known Mudungazi since childhood. And I know that debauched woman who goes by the name Damboia. I don't want to waste your time; you've come a long way. You can kill me."

Pieces of straw rose from a nearby hut. They quivered in the calm air and landed on the ground. Two birds sliced through the sky. A child cried. The mother smothered the cry. Mafemane was smiling. Maguiguane wanted to raise his spear. He wasn't able to do it. His hand felt heavy. Mputa remained in the same position, impassive. Mafemane was smiling. The sun was descending, red. Minutes passed. The silence weighed down. The night was approaching.

From the end of the corridor, a spear cut through the air and thrust itself into Mafemane's chest. Mafemane, tall as he was, threw his body backward and returned to his initial position, fixing his eyes on Ualalapi, who was running away.

"Who is that?" asked Mafemane.

"It's Ualalapi," answered the nearest warriors.

"Call him. He must finish me, as the laws order. Where is he from?"

"He is Nguni."

"Ah!" he sighed, smiling. His body began to bend. As his spine folded forward, the spear thrust deeper into his bloody chest. He returned, with some effort, to his initial position and spat a gob of blood. His knees moved closer to the ground and settled on it definitively seconds later. He dug his hands into the sand and remained in the genuflective position for a good few seconds, waiting for Ualalapi, who was approaching with his head bowed. The pain in Mafemane's chest was such that he fell on his back, directing his eyes to the sky, where three stars were beginning to shine. Without the courage to look at him, Ualalapi approached Mafemane, knelt, took the spear out of his chest, and thrust it in again, countless times. The face, the chest, and other parts of Ualalapi's body became covered in hot blood, thrown out by Mafemane's body, already dead. And as the blood was running over Ualalapi's body, he squeezed his eyes even tighter and thrust the spear with ever greater fury into the perforated chest, destroyed, unrecognizable. Maguiguane and Mputa approached.

"That's enough," they said. "He died long ago."

Ualalapi held the spear a few inches from Mafemane's chest and stood up. He wiped the spear with his left hand and began to run, passing through the houses of the village and shouting a strident, heartrending "No!," such as no one had ever heard. He disappeared into the forest covered by the night, breaking with his body the leaves and branches his blood-filled eyes did not see. Minutes later, the cry of a woman and a child joined the "No!" and the sound of the forest being torn apart. And the same sound covered the sky and the land for eleven days and eleven nights, the same time in years as the rule of Ngungunhane, the name adopted by Mudungazi on ascending to emperorship of the lands of Gaza.

FRAGMENTS FROM THE END (2)

> *Handwritten annotation:*
> • One part where the port are being represented outside a quote
> • fictionalized

Feeling that it was standing on a strange and hard object, the horse lifted its front hooves, neighed, and stamped them over the body again, precisely on the thin and soft stomach of the black man.

The black man screamed, dug his hands into the moist sand, opened his eyes extraordinarily wide, expelled a gush of blood from his mouth, and saw his guts coming out, perforated by bullets.

Colonel Galhardo looked at the black man, saw his guts draining onto the earth, saw the intestinal liquids disappearing into the trampled grass, saw the blood draining over the body, and was not moved. He looked again at the black man's face and noted that the man was trying to raise his head. The sinews of his neck were strained, tense.

"Where is the king?" he asked.

The black man again opened his eyes very wide, tried to dig with his fingers with greater force, slowly raised his head, spat a new gob of blood from his mouth, and finally let his head fall again onto the ground. The colonel looked at the blood dripping from the horse's front hooves, looked at the face disfigured by death, and commented with a faint smile on his lips:

"These niggers have the strength of a horse!"

He reined in his horse, turned it to the left, and contemplated with a slight weariness the sea of unburied dead bodies displayed on the plain. In the distance, in silence, the capital of the empire of Gaza rose. Its drab houses were falling asleep in the fleeing afternoon.

"Burn the village," ordered the colonel and spurred his horse on in the direction of the nearest hillock.

MPUTA'S DEATH

For Segone Ndangalila · for Magambo · and for Misete

And the Lord, answering Job out of the whirlwind, said:
Who is this that hideth counsel without knowledge?
Where wast thou when I laid the foundations of the earth?
Will the eagle mount up at thy command, and make her nest in high places?
Then Job answered the Lord, and said:
I know that thou canst do all things, and no thought is hid from thee …
Therefore I reprehend myself, and do penance in dust and ashes.

Job 38:42

Waking up on that misty and inauspicious morning, Domia felt her innards churning in a frightening and deadly way, but she did not worry too much because she knew that such pain always came when she thought of the details of the act she had been planning for years, since the day her father, whose name was Mputa, had been killed and chopped into pieces because the queen, first wife of Ngungunhane, called inkosikazi in these lands, accused him of uttering words so harmful that tears came to her face as she repeated them, between sobs, to the king, who swore in the name of his grandfather, Manicusse, that Mputa, dog without name and history, would kiss the earth forever and ever because words of such wickedness were not permitted in his kingdom, and even less to the wife of a king to whom the subjects owed respect by all means possible; and, saying this with abundant gestures and a contorted face, he sent the *chitopo,* the name given to the town crier of the kingdom, to call together a large gathering, which should meet that same morning without fail or excuses because an affront to his wife was an insult to himself, king of vast lands, and to all the people of his empire, who owe to him the dignity and pride of being men, because it was me and all of my predecessors who banished the endless night that was covering these lands, he was saying while moving his big-bellied body through the atrium of the royal house and pointing with his hands and directing his eyes to the clouds, the sun, and the majestic trees growing in the distance, to his wife who was sobbing, and to the chitopo who was following him, nodding his head for everything and for nothing, did you hear, vassal, I gave the light and the smile, I gave the meat and the wine, I gave the joy to these worms, and it won't be this dog, a man to whom I gave the honor of cooking for me, the one to dare raise his voice, so go, run, I want them now, and if you find someone defecating take him from the shit, and if he is glued to his wife, take him from the embrace with the power that the empire gives you; I am, and will be forever and always, Ngungunhane, as was wanted by my parents and grandparents and all the descendants of the Nguni heroes who raised these lands from the lethargy of nameless centuries, go servant, go call them, tear them away from where they are and bring them to the big tree, and you, woman, mother of all the mothers, clean the tears that furrow your face, because before the moon appears you will be smiling at the tragic death that filthy animal, son of dogs, will have.

The elite of the kingdom exchanged glances, uneasy because they did not know who had taken the buffalo by the horns, as the common folk say; and while the king was digging into the honeycomb until he reached the honey, the nobles of the kingdom relaxed, stretched their legs, rested their bodies, and followed with greater attention the words that were coming down the steps of the kingdom and striking against the common folk, those men without name and purpose. Then, more confident in their knowledge that the words were fleeing from the center, they nodded their heads to the rhythm of the wrathful words that fell in disarray, until, to the relief and pleasure of all except Molungo, the name of Mputa arose in the airs of the morning. And when the sovereign passed the death penalty on the dirty Tsonga dog, the elite moved their eyes and heads in a sign of unanimous approval.

Molungo, uncle of the sovereign, the man who would accompany the king in the misfortune of endless years of exile, asked to speak, knowing that Mputa could not have committed such a crime because many were the times that he had seen the inkosikazi circling the man like an animal in heat, but dammit, he was thinking, a king cannot go back on his word, and it would not be him, Molungo, who would turn over the mountain; but he had, to his pleasure, the power to reduce the sentence handed down, and that is why he began to praise the king, filling the testicles, big belly, and enormous bum of the hosi with possible and imagined glories, with real and unreal facts of which he, king of so many deeds, hero without equal in history, was the first and only protagonist, to be recorded by history for as long as men remain on the earth!

This being said in an overexcited voice, as is right for flattery, the sovereign did nothing but nod his head, showing his teeth eaten away by snuff and alcohol, and allowing Molungo to lance the abscess. With the astuteness that life had taught him, Molungo said to the king in a kind of synthesis that death is not appropriate for a man who dared to desire the queen's body. A punishment both brutal and memorable in the minds of the subjects was necessary; why not blind him as the Tsongas used to do in the times not worth remembering? If you do this, your imperial power will emerge with greater strength in these tumultuous times in which men the color of skinned goats are besieging your vast empire. Blind him, emperor, in front of his own kind, and you will see that this formless mass will become delirious because no other method will make them rejoice as much as the tradition that in times gone by these worms used to follow religiously!

Molungo sat down, knowing that honey is sweet on its own and that Mputa would be man enough to remove the web that enveloped him.

You went for the gut, said the king, pleased with such praise; and the others, the elite of the kingdom, again moved their eyes and bodies in a sign of unanimous consent and asked the king to blind Mputa in front of his own kind.

The king ordered that the chitopo be informed to sound the *chipalapala* horn and call the Tsongas of the surrounding areas so that they could represent all the people of the empire, which stretches from the Limpopo to the Zambezi. As he said this, he stood up and began to walk in the direction of his house, thinking and rethinking the speech that would stir even the most skeptical, while the elite of the kingdom returned to their houses, commenting on what they already should have commented, without paying attention to the progressing afternoon and even less to the sound that floated in the air, alarming the species asleep for centuries, stirring waters unmoved since the creation of the world and men in whose forgotten graves unknown plants were growing and multiplying, forming impenetrable bush where the most recent spirits were resting from the human and animal agitation, while following, with a smile never seen before, the barbarities committed by men for infantile reasons invented and nourished for centuries on end!

"Mputa forgot that the storm brings rain, son. The king's wife is sacred."

"Why, grandfather? What does she have between her thighs that no other woman has?"

"Don't say that, son, don't say that, because years ago, before your father was born, there was a man who dared to throw unheard-of insults at the king, and this man spent the rest of his life missing his testicles. Don't say that. Leave Mputa. Leave him! He forgot that whoever stirs the pond raises the mud."

"But doesn't clucking mean an egg was laid, grandfather?"

"Don't say anything else, let's be quiet. If Mputa is right, he will leave unhurt because the monkey does not let himself be defeated by the tree."

And it was in this atmosphere of commentary, peculiar to the common folk, that Ngungunhane appeared before the crowd, with his loincloth of animal skins and decorative tails, accompanied by the elite of the kingdom and by Mputa, flanked by royal guards, in the midst of the tam-tam that reverberated from the dried skins like sounds coming from the innards, carrying on for centuries, thundering through the afternoon without clouds, beautiful, immaculate. And when the silence returned, the sovereign, with the pride inherited by the Shangaan, calmly addressed the crowd, saying that Mputa is a hut without grass. He surprised the rabbit and did not have the courage to run after it. These were his first words, which drove the Tsonga people to delirium. They had forgotten they were facing the invader who had settled in those lands with the blood of innocent warriors never remembered, and everyone, except Domia, who was at the back of the crowd with tears imprisoned in her childlike eyes, exhorted the sovereign to kill the man who not long ago had placed at the king's feet the heads of five lions killed with a knife in close combat. The words excited them so much that when the king asked whether or not he should give the criminal Mputa, animal like the Chope, the right to speak, many had doubts and others refused him that right. The king smiled, saying afterward that he would give the dog the right to speak, despite him not having any such right because dogs are dogs!

Mputa, with his athletic body, came before the crowd and spoke in such a calm tone that the silence reigned, as in the sleepy hours of the siesta.

"You can kill me, king, you can tear me to pieces. You have imperial power, which has weighed in your body since you were born. But I, a vassal like all those you see in front of you, have done nothing, said nothing to the inkosikazi. This is my truth. I know that you doubt this because the word of the inkosikazi is sacred in your ears and the ears of all your subjects. You can kill me, king, because long ago it was said that I would die in this innocent way. But before you kill me, I ask of you to submit me to the *mondzo,* so that my innocence can be proven to the people."

And he said nothing more because his eyes, with an indescribable shine, carried all the truth his words were not able to express. And those who had the courage to look into his eyes lived afflicted by insomnia because they felt like accomplices in a crime.

In view of Mputa's clear words, the king had to turn to his adviser because the doubt, which should never affect the sovereign in public, penetrated his body with such intensity that his hands shook. The people, in silence, no longer knew where to turn their heads. The king couldn't do otherwise but accept Mputa's wish to submit to the mondzo, the name given to the ordeal by poison prepared in those lands of the empire.

And it was in a sepulchral silence that Mputa drank the mondzo without blinking, without moving a muscle of his body. And so he remained for endless minutes, face to face with the incredulity of the people and of the kingdom's nobles, who were staring at him, black and shining in his loincloth of animal skin, at the dying of the day, with the sun beating down on his chest, his protruding veins, and his knotted hair.

He is a witch, said the king with an unheard-of firmness. And witches have no place in my kingdom. I will not blind him as you wished me to do, because witches work in the mist of the night. I will kill him today and now! And he turned to the guards, who pushed Mputa to the middle of the crowd.

The thirteen-year-old Domia saw her father being beaten and hacked into pieces by the royal guards and by some elements of the population, because others, aware of Mputa's innocence, left the area, trying to forget what they never would forget.

After tidying her things, Domia left her hut, straightened her skirt whipped by the wind, which was announcing the rain that would tumble down at the moment of her death, and began to walk in the direction of the royal house, doubtful of her action after four years of waiting. She knew she was going to die. Something inside her was announcing her death, a terrible death.

Ngungunhane, leaning against the covering of the house that reached the ground, indifferent to the wind of misfortune, was smoking *mbhangui,* the name given to cannabis, much smoked by the Tsonga people, and thinking about the calamity that afflicted his house, as for more than four weeks his thirty wives, spread throughout the capital, had been pouring blood down their thighs, an unprecedented fact in his married and polygamous life, when he saw Domia crossing the enclosure to his house.

"What are you coming to do at this time?"

"Clean your house, hosi?"

The king looked at her, saw the curve of her hips, her chest, and her breasts rising from the piece of cloth that was trying to cover them.

"What's your name?"

"Domia, my lord."

"Domia... Do you know who Domia was?"

"I know, hosi. She was the mother of Mawewe, brother and rival of your father, Muzila."

"Don't call that dog my brother! And for what reason did your father give you that name?"

Domia lowered her eyes and said nothing. The king ordered her to enter his house. As the door was low, she had to bend down and enter on her hands and knees. The emperor followed her with his eyes and then entered.

Seeing her as she stood shaking, Ngungunhane tore off the piece of cloth that was covering her breasts and pulled her toward him with the fury of an animal that had not seen the opposite sex for a long time. Domia took the knife out of her skirt and waited for the right moment. That was her mistake.

She thought, and justifiably so, that the king would push her against the wall and would do everything standing, because she had never imagined that the sovereign would take a servant to the bed where the queens used to lie down. That is what he did, after having seen the shining tip of the knife during their passage indoors.

"Do you want to kill me?" asked the king, to which she did not answer, because she tried immediately to plunge the knife into the emperor's chest. He pushed her hand away and felt the knife penetrate his right thigh. He did not pay attention to it. He took the knife out of the girl's hand and brutally possessed her, she underneath and he on top, she kicking her legs and trying to hit him, and he panting and trying to crush her with the weight of man and king.

Violated and wounded inside, and with her plans foiled, Domia did nothing but spit in the face of the king and call him dog, something that nobody had had the courage to say to his face since the king was born, because he knew they were saying everything behind his back, but to his face, never! And he shook. He shook on seeing Domia's shining eyes, glowing in the windowless house like the eyes of an enraged cat. He shook on feeling degraded as sovereign. He shook on realizing that the word fell from the mouth of a woman. He shook on understanding that the girl was Mputa's daughter. And he shook on seeing the mocking smile appear on the girl's lips.

Minutes later Domia was taken away by the royal guards, with categorical orders to make her disappear from the face of the earth.

When the rain beat down, Domia gave her last breath, leaving her flesh to be decomposed by the rain, which did not stop falling for weeks and weeks, until not a bone was left on the earth. And the king spent the rest of his life contemplating, alone, the furrow that would never be erased from his body, no matter what.

And few were those who knew that Ngungunhane had an indelible mark on the right thigh of his body.

FRAGMENTS FROM THE END (3)

"The orders of Your Excellency have been carried out. The column under my command completed the march on Manjacaze. Having arrived at the coastal plain, I provoked the enemy into combat, bombarding the village. Ngungunhane's people appeared in the bush that surrounds and hides the kraal, in small groups, answering only with some rifle shots to the artillery fire of the column, which dispersed them rapidly."

"Then, leaving the convoy properly escorted, I marched to Manjacaze, which I found abandoned, but with a lot of munitions and objects used by the inhabitants, everything in the disorder characteristic of a hurried flight. The auxiliaries plundered the village and the kinglet's *chigocho,* which soon afterward I ordered to be torched, leaving everything completely destroyed and returning with the column to the bivouac on the coastal plain."

Thus began Colonel Galhardo's report to posterity. It is a detailed and long-winded report, but it fails in important respects omitted by the colonel, who did not record:

—The fact of having profaned the *Ihambelo* like a heathen, urinating with some effort over the platform where Ngungunhane used to speak in times of the rituals, not to mention the spittle mixed with the tobacco of the cigar held between the colonel's scorched lips, which he squirted at the log wall.

—The theft of five lion skins, which he exhibited in Lisbon, claiming they came from a dangerous hunt in African lands.

—The fact of having personally disemboweled five blacks with the purpose of verifying the size of the niggers' hearts.

—The fact of having remained serious and serene as he faced the flames that were consuming the huts of the empire's capital, and listened to the cry of a child in flames who was crawling, in despair, between the flames and the burnt logs and the grass and the tumbling adobe walls, looking for life in the stupidity of war.

About this man, the then royal commissioner of Mozambique (1895), António Enes, wrote the following some years later in his memoirs: If in the gallery of illustrious men, bravery, tenacity, respect for mankind, kindness, and love of the fatherland are recorded, Colonel Galhardo's merit has earned him a well-deserved place there.

DAMBOIA

For Anibal Aleluia

As much as she hath glorified herself, and lived in delicacies, so much torment and sorrow give ye to her; because she saith in her heart: I sit a queen, and am no widow; and sorrow I shall not see. Therefore shall her plagues come in one day, death, and mourning, and famine, and she shall be burnt with the fire; because God is strong, who shall judge her.

Revelation 18

I

With the exception of the day, the time, and other small details, everyone was unanimous in affirming that Damboia, the youngest sister of Muzila, died of a never-ending menstruation after three months of living with her thighs darkened by viscous and foul-smelling blood that flowed in continuous gushes, impeding her from moving farther than the entrance of her house, located a few yards from the residence of the emperor of these lands of Gaza, who, by his order, put around Damboia's house royal guards charged with preventing intruding looks and also burning aromatic plants, which did not succeed in removing the nauseating odor of blood that covered the village during those fateful months in which the *nkuaia* (annual and sacred ritual in which the subjects from all corners of the empire came to the court singing and offering delicacies and other diverse things to the sovereign of sovereigns, who accepted everything, in the midst of the hymns of praise to the emperor, who on the last day of the month went to the lhambelo, the name given to the sacred place, nude and accompanied, for the rituals that culminated in the killing of cattle and two young people, of both sexes, who were put into the magical dish that would invigorate the empire and give everyone strength for the drinking that would follow and for the following morning's *untento*, where everything was discussed with the protocol and moderation of language as in the present parliaments and assemblies) did not take place, despite being in a year of uprisings and wars, because the woman of the court was afflicted by a strange disease, never seen in these lands since the time when another woman, named Misiui, poured milk from her breasts for years without end, filling pitchers and barrels and bringing people from distant villages and impenetrable marshes to visit her with the expectant curiosity of seeing a barren woman, with breasts the size of grains of corn, who was talking to everybody and supplying milk for children and sick and dying old people.

But this happened in times gone by and did not affect a woman of the court such as Damboia. Because of this, said Ngungunhane, she was more important than the affairs of the empire, and as long as I am alive, gatherings don't need to happen; I represent everybody: men, women, old people, and children of this endless empire; this he said with all his power concentrated in his voice, as if thousands of vassals inhabited his fat body, which he showed off to everybody and which flourished from day to day with the infinite responsibilities given to him by the empire, as he solved them with his voice and his gestures, because there was no paper and the orders were written by the thunderous voice that reverberated in the rainy and dry mornings and afternoons.

I sent heralds through this empire to make it known, he said, that Damboia is suffering from a terminal illness, contracted in the service of the empire that her hands helped to build, and all, chiefs and subjects, lords and vassals, must ask their distant and recent ancestors to save her from this incurable disease, as they had done for that servant named Mfussi, who could not see anything around her but red and black serpents entwining her, day and night, wherever she went. And it will not be with Damboia, a woman of the court and not a vassal like that Mfussi and others, that the voice of the spirits will not exorcise the evils she suffers from. Save her from this misfortune, which does not affect just her but everyone, and if she goes, the empire goes, men!

And because of this and further things that you may wish to say, for the good of the kingdom, the nkuaia will not take place. The hymns of praise that rejuvenate us will not reverberate in the capital. The warriors will not beat their shields in the *bayete* salute, raising the prehistoric dust of our forgotten ancestors. The sun and the clouds will not take on the color of the days of victory, and the wind will not bring the indelible voice of the Nguni heroes. So, the laws that have been in force until now will stay in force, and I will be the man from whom more laws will come when needed, because the empire is mine and power belongs to me. Go, vassals, and douse the torches that have been burning throughout this empire. And so that the Chope don't laugh at our pain, you, Maguiguane, go through these lands spreading death and pain. I want everyone, but everyone, to sympathize with the suffering that has assailed us. Go, warriors, as the empire protects you, now and after death.

II

Opinions differ about the day on which Damboia, leaning on the doorpost of her house, felt the sticky blood running down her thighs, a foreboding of the never-ending moonlight of her death.

Malule, who had been guarding the stricken house from intrusive gazes, had told me that on that day the tops of the trees were stripped by the accursed wind which came carrying shells from the immeasurable depths of the distant sea. The afternoon was falling. The houses were crying. And the men, shaking, collected everything essential that they had outside their huts, entered the houses that were groaning with the wind, and waited for the night, imploring the spirits for an immediate end to that accursed wind. The night arrived. In the sky, there were shining stars and a sickle moon. There were no clouds. And the wind, growing in intensity, took the roofs off the poorest houses and exposed to the night of the spirits the poverty of homeless and nameless men of all the centuries.

At the breaking of day, a heavy yellow rain began to fall in large and clammy drops like the slime of a snail. For seven days and seven nights, the populations of the outskirts of Mandlakazi, the name given to the capital of the empire, felt that abnormal rain on their skin. In the royal village, there were sun and a calm wind. In the first days, it was normal to see Ngungunhane making his way to the outskirts, accompanied by the elite of the kingdom, contemplating that sour rain and appealing for calm; everything will be all right, the gazelle doesn't dance with happiness in two places at once, men, calm is needed, lots of calm.

Those who wished to take refuge in the royal village received a whipping from the guard. And with reason, because nobody knew what sicknesses they were carrying, dirty as they were, covered in that grimy sludge, like snot. The king was right to push them away. He had to live forever and ever, even at the expense of all his subjects' lives.

On the fourth day, the men of the court sought refuge in their houses and gave up appearing in the street. A strange phenomenon was taking place in the outskirts: Corpses without name and face appeared on the surface of the muddy water, if that viscous and thick liquid could be called water. Tinomba, chief of the adjacent village, went from house to house of the settlement, counting those who were alive and asking about the dead, who were unknown to everybody, for three days and three nights, which was equal to the time of the permanence of the corpses, which mysteriously disappeared with the end of the rain, on the seventh night, making the witch doctors state that those corpses were from other forgotten times and had come as a warning to those people who respected nothing and gossiped about all they had heard and hadn't heard.

On the last Saturday of the third month of pain, Damboia died. On the following day, the five strongest men of the area woke up impotent for the rest of their lives. And that was not the most important thing to happen during all those months. The worst thing that happened during those months were the words, man! They were growing minute by minute and entering all the houses, flinging open doors and walls, and changing their sound according to the people they found. The violence that Ngungunhane used to stop them had no effect. They were covering distances at the speed of the wind. And all this because of those *tinhloco*—the Tsonga name for servants—who were leaving Damboia's house with bags full of words they were throwing to the wind. Bitches! Who has ever heard of a faceless individual cursing a person of the court, a woman we all served with respect and love? Whores, beasts without name, they were the ones carrying invented histories in their bags, saying that Damboia was suffering from an illness in her chest that causes the vomiting of blood from the mouth, but that she was vomiting from between her thighs because of the filthy life she had led.

"Filthy?"

"Don't pay attention. These are words of the commoners. They have no basis in fact. Damboia had the most perfect life that I ever knew."

"Where there's smoke, there's fire, Malule."

"You will never find water scratching a rock. Let me talk. I know the truth. I lived in the court."

"But what man has no snot in his nose, Malule?"

"If Damboia had faults, they were not substantial. She knew men, like any other woman. And that's none of our business. The roof of the house knows the owner."

"But the snail leaves a trail of slime when it passes."

"Everything you heard around here is lies. From the mouth of these people only the feelers of the snail appear. They invent stories, spread words, sleep with them, defecate them all over the place. It's all lies. I lived at the court . . ."

"Even if you walk on the lower path, the hunchback can still be seen, Malule."

His eyes glittered in the night. He put two logs on the dying fire and refused to open his mouth. I didn't insist.

III

Ciliane, who had been Damboia's servant, told me a different version in her hoarse voice marked by old age, saying first of all that on that ominous day Damboia had lived the happiest moments of her life.

In the morning, Damboia spoke with the witch doctor, who observed, among other things, that royalty is not common, vassalage is common, a warning she chose not to heed, enchanted as she was by the sunny morning trickling down through the gigantic and tiny trees, while birds of a thousand colors were singing never-written melodies. Having left the witch doctor's house, she began wandering, swaying her well-fleshed buttocks, picking up and dropping brown and green leaves, laughing at everything and nothing, until she crossed paths with Ciliane, who was coming with a pitcher in the right hand of her young body, tired from so much work done and yet to be done until old age, when women drag themselves to the fires to tell never-ending stories, like the one Ciliane told me about Damboia, the evil-tempered and filthy woman of Ngungunhane's court.

"Where are you going, Ciliane?" asked Damboia.

"To the river."

"Let's go together," she said, walking along, she on the right and Ciliane on the left, on endless paths lined with centuries-old plants that did not grow more than three feet high. Ciliane transferred the pitcher from her right hand to her left and looked fixedly at her feet, without knowing what to say to Damboia, who was smiling and looking at the birds slicing through the sky.

"Did you know that Mosheshe's wife went into the marsh, followed by her young children?" asked Ciliane, looking at Damboia's ankles, wrapped with beads sparkling in the sun.

"No, I didn't know. Why did she do that?" she replied, uninterested.

"She couldn't stand seeing you."

"She's brave . . . And what's being said about it?"

"The usual words: you are a bitch."

"But why, Ciliane? What wrong have I done to them?"

"You killed men, Damboia. You killed Sidulo, Mosheshe, Sigugo, and others."

"And who has not killed, Ciliane?" her eyes fell on Ciliane, keen and piercing.

"Many."

"You lie. We all kill. You have already killed me in several ways."

"Me, no. I never thought about your death. I limit myself to repeating what is being said. And it is they who say you killed honest and innocent men."

"Don't make me laugh."

"That's what they say . . ."

"Have you ever refused to obey the orders of your master?"

"Never."

"They refused to obey my orders."

"But what orders, Damboia? Don't you think it's human for a man to refuse to go to bed with a woman?"

"Who were they to refuse my orders? People of the street, without name, people who never dreamed of crossing the door of my house. If they were men of their word, they would have refused me at the moment when I pointed at them."

"They were afraid of you."

"And why did they stop fearing me?"

"Only you can know that . . . Before dying, Mosheshe was supposed to have said, according to what I was told, that those who took him from the world of the living would have a terrible death."

"Was he referring to me?"

"It was you who killed him."

"I ordered him to be killed, that's different. But he was not the first. Sidulo stated in my presence that maggots would infest my body while I was alive."

"Days dawn with different colors, Damboia."

"It's possible, but I came from far away, Ciliane. The worst days will come with old age, which I hate."

They fell silent, looking at the waters of the river that was running through the plain, wriggling its shiny hips. Damboia took off her clothes and jumped into the water. She looked pretty, said Ciliane, pushing a log into the fire. It was an indescribable, serene beauty. I think that death had already entered that slender body. As the afternoon approached, she ran through the royal village, playing with the children she never had. She was greeting everyone who crossed her path. At dusk, she placed herself at the entrance of her house and contemplated the sinking sun, all red. It was Friday. Mosheshe had been dead for two weeks. I remember she was supposed to have said that day had been the best day of her life. She was radiant. When the sun set, she felt the blood running and limited herself to saying, without worrying too much, that her regular timing was off. She entered her hut and never left it alive again. And it was only in the deepest night, if I remember well, that she asked for me. There were no stars in the sky. There was no moon. The wind was calm. When I entered, on my knees, I felt my hands slipping in a muddy sludge. I thought it was water, but it wasn't. The ground was soaked with blood, and Damboia was standing, serene as always. She directed her eyes at the ground and pointed with her hands. I spent the whole night cleaning the ground. At the break of day, I noticed that the blood was ankle deep. Damboia's capulana wrap was soaked with blood. The walls were dyed red. The hovering smell was the same as what women had on certain days of the month. And I was tired. Damboia was not saying anything. Whoever saw her in that position, erect, distant, might say that she was thinking about the ancestors she had never known. Standing, with my body also covered in blood, I was waiting for her to say something. "Go call Ngungunhane," she said, answering my thoughts.

When I left the hut, I noticed that the sun had the same colors as always. The trees were in the same place, and the birds were warbling songs known since the beginning of all time. The old people were drifting along, tasting the morning. The women were stoking the fires, and the children were running, cheerful. The world was in the same place, a fact that astonished me.

The conversation she had with Ngungunhane took hours, and nobody found out what they had talked about. Afterward I learned that the nkuaia would not take place. This decision was not appreciated by the elders because the nkuaia only fails to take place in the year in which the king dies. Damboia was not the sovereign and she was not dead. But soon the elders got used to the idea, and the days passed. I remember that when I brought more tinhloco slaves to clean the floor and take care of Damboia, the house was surrounded by guards and the entrance was flooded with blood, which the earth was refusing to absorb. The pitchers broke into pieces when we tried to fill them with blood. We chose to cover the blood with sand. And the blood, to the surprise of everyone, was continually reappearing, until it was ankle deep. Damboia was not speaking, just looking. And it was only at the end of the first month that she tried to open her mouth again. The words did not come. The madness invaded her. She began to crawl and climb the walls of the house, like a reptile in despair. During the night, she howled like the dogs. Many of the guards surrounding the house became deaf for the rest of their lives, and others have had attacks of madness from time to time, such as Malule, with whom you talked yesterday. Others, unable to bear that stench, abandoned their weapons and went deep into the forest, in search of death. The king called the famous witch doctors of the area, but they could do little. There was one, however, that remained for days and days speaking a language no one could understand, and the only thing he managed to do was bring Damboia to her senses on the last Thursday of every month. On those days, the blood stopped flowing and she spoke with everybody, oblivious to the drama of her life. As you can see, she had two days of sanity in those three months. And for many that was the worst thing the witch doctor did, because when night came the howls began again with brutal intensity, and the blood was falling like a waterfall.

During the second month, I think, it rained as never before for two weeks. Her blood ran to the river, colored it red, and killed the fish, which the Nguni did not eat. The crocodiles began to live on the banks of the river. It was normal to see them at the threshold of our doors at the break of day. In the beginning, we tried to chase them away, but they came in greater numbers, in the thousands. Some old people committed suicide. Others, old and young, died of thirst because the water was contaminated along the course of the river. The nearby lake was contaminated. And the few wells that existed were reserved for the people of the court. Ngungunhane walked to and fro, insisting that all was well in the empire and that there were major improvements, because harvests that never happened filled the granaries with endless bounty, and the children who were never born came into the world fatter and healthier, and the old people lived longer, and the warriors were winning more battles. Those who spoke to the contrary were hanged from the trees. Everybody is happy, and if the nkuaia does not take place, it is because Damboia is sick, men, he said, roaring with his hands and raising his voice. If anything must torment us, it is Damboia's illness. And we spent all those months hearing his words in every corner. Every day people were dying, but it was said that they were dying from old age. Those who committed suicide were mentally ill, individuals attacked by evil spirits. And the months were passing by. And it was on the last Thursday of the third month of pain that Damboia, in the middle of the night, gave the most piercing howl that had been heard during those months. She died. On the following morning it began to rain, and on the flooded ground the stillborn children of women who always dreamed of having children appeared. And it was terrible having to tread on those bodies that were decomposing at our feet.

Ngungunhane, thin and voiceless, went around like a lost sleepwalker, smoking mbhangui at all hours.

FRAGMENTS FROM THE END (4)

As soon as the niggers ran away, I saw a man wearing a crown emerge from a nearby hut, and I asked him about Gungunhana; he pointed me to the same hut from which he had come out. I called Gungunhana's name very loudly in the midst of absolute silence, preparing myself to set the hut alight in case he delayed too long, when I saw the Vatua kinglet leaving, whom the lieutenants Miranda and Couto immediately recognized because they had seen him more than once in Manjacase. The arrogance with which he answered the first questions I asked him was unfathomable. I ordered one of the two black soldiers to tie his hands behind his back, and I told him to sit down. He asked me where, and as I pointed to the ground, he responded very haughtily that it was dirty. I then forced him to sit on the ground (something he never used to do) and told him that he was no longer the king of the Mangonis but a Matonga like any other.

I asked Gungunhana about Queto, Manhune, Molungo, and Maguiguana. He pointed out Queto and Manhune, who stood next to him, and said that the others were not there.

I upbraided Manhune (who was the damned soul of Gungunhana) for always having been an enemy of the Portuguese, to which he answered only that he knew he had to die. I then ordered him to be bound to a stake of the palisade, and he was shot by three whites. It is not possible to die with more cold blood, pride, and true heroism; he just said, smiling, that it would be better to untie him so he could fall when he was shot. Then it was Queto. He was the only brother of Muzila who had chosen to fight against us and the only one who had been at the battle of Coolela. He had not come to surrender, as his brothers, Inguiusa and Cuiu, had done.

When I told him this, he answered that he could not abandon Gungunhana, whom he had raised as if he had been his father; and I retorted that whoever disobeyed and went to war against the King of Portugal ought to be abandoned by father, mother, and brothers. I ordered him also to be tied and shot.

Extracts from the report presented to Counsellor Correia e Lança, acting governor of the Province of Mozambique, by the military governor of Gaza, Joaquim Mouzinho de Albuquerque (1896)

A SIEGE OR FRAGMENTS OF A SIEGE

For Wantamele

I

On entering the tenth day of the siege, the warriors looked at everything with and without life that the earth had carried since the beginning of the beginnings and arrived at the sad conclusion that the world had lost its centuries-old beauty and vigor. The sky and the earth took on the color of disemboweled bodies. Days succeeded days at the pace of senile sleepwalkers. Rain clouds were passing in the distance, and a soft breeze was exhaling sad songs of distinguished warriors killed in virile battles, with spears crossing in the air and shields clashing thunderously against each other in the grass ravaged by men and by the hymns of victory that reverberated over the plain covered with dead bodies and hissing snakes, driven crazy by the infernal vision that was rising on the plain.

Now, deprived of the vigor of their ancestors, the warriors grew old in the shade of gray trees, seeing their spears form peaks of loneliness and their shields being used as nests by mice.

11

Maguiguane was then, since the enthronement of Ngungunhane, the military chief of the emperor of the lands of Gaza. In the first days of the siege, it was normal to see him talking with the warriors in several camps. Then, overpowered by the torpor of the mornings and afternoons, he closed himself in his hut and spent the hours listening for signs of change. At night, and only at night, would he dare to leave the hut. He dressed himself in his war clothes, adorning his head with plumes of feathers, picked up his spear and shield, looked at himself from head to toe, left the hut, and walked in the direction of Macanhangana, his lieutenant, who was waiting for him in the same place and at the same time.

"Incredible!"

"Yes, in the same place and at the same time since the first day of the siege of the fort of Chirrime, where Chope king Binguane and his son Xipenanyane were surrounded, with the women and the children. And the warriors, obviously. The two did not greet each other. Maguiguane just looked at his lieutenant and walked ahead. They would walk in silence through the main camp, listening to the spent laughs and stories with known variations, treading on the same places, contemplating the same huts, the usual bushes, the sky of the same color, the stars without brilliance, and the gray and sickle moon. They left the main camp by the same path, went down the short slope, bypassed the usual cliff, approached the well, looked with the same intensity as always at the warriors talking near the fire, moved on in the direction of the fort, which was referred to by the generic name of *nkocolene,* and walked alongside it from one end to the other. As they strolled, they avoided, in the same places, the scattered feces and the drunken vomit and the lakes of piss that were a breeding place for fish without fins or eyes. Once they had completed the walk along the encirclement, they returned to the usual path and went up the small ladder that took them to the courtyard with scattered trees and trembling fires. Macanhangana broke the silence, saying his everyday words in the same deep and distant tone of every day:

'They won't last.'

'It's true, they won't last,' replied Maguiguane and went in the direction of his hut. Minutes later, Macanhangana was doing the same."

III

Night. The hyenas howl. The snakes hiss. The men dream. The owls hoot. The mosquitoes buzz, fly into the huts, fling themselves at the flesh, suck the blood; one dies, another flings itself against the log wall, and others wait: feeling the hot blood in the air, they buzz, they bite, they live, they die.

There is a false, veiled silence. The flames lose their strength in the deserted yard. The wind lifts scattered leaves. The booming of the thunder can be heard in the distance, very far away. It rains in the capital of the empire. Macanhangana drinks *sope* liquor, drinks interminably. He fears the night. He sees the walls of the hut shaking. He feels the house undulating. He clings to his straw bed. His eyes shine. Two tears jump out. He cries. The owls hoot. The wind timidly raises the straw of the huts. Maguiguane thinks of the king. The king thinks of his concubine, Vuiazi, mother of Godide, who mysteriously disappeared with her buttocks, her body, her smile, her soft black, shining face. Vuiazi thinks of Kamal Samade, the Arab trader who confined himself to the marshes of Inhafura because he was accused of sleeping with Vuiazi. Maguiguane falls asleep. He dreams of the same thing. He sees snakes cowardly devouring the men, thousands of men. The women remain, tearful, lost on the plain. The warriors snore. The guards scrutinize the night. They feel hyenas approaching. They see the glow of their eyes. The starved look. The stumbling step. The moon disappears in a passing cloud. Macanhangana clutches his straw bed; he wants to vomit, he cannot; he looks at the ceiling, he sees the stars without brilliance between the gaps in the straw. Maguiguane snores. The king dreams aloud, he calls for Vuiazi, he clings to his decorated straw bed; he sweats, farts, coughs, ejaculates. Vuiazi thinks of the sodomy of Kamal Samade, sickness and vice unknown in those lands of Gaza. The night flees. The warriors fear the morning, the sun, the wind of forgotten hymns, the earth without color, the trees with wilted leaves, the sky without clouds, the dead plain.

IV

"What is the meaning of this dream?"

"The lion roars in the jungle, Maguiguane."

"And the women, Mabuiau, the women?"

The same dialogue. The unchanging words. The gestures of every day.

Maguiguane wakes up with a start. Rolls his eyes repeatedly. He sees no snakes. He sees threads of light falling on the floor. He raises himself, resting on his elbows. He sees his body cut across by the light. He stands up. He caresses his spear. Mabuiau enters, sits in the circle of light. Waits. Maguiguane relates his dream. Asks questions. Listens to the answers. Mabuiau leaves. The morning grows. Maguiguane approaches the wall and waits for the signs of change. Macanhangana sleeps deeply. The warriors stretch, walk toward the same trees, sit in the same shade, and tell the same stories. Those who are listening try to forget the initial plot. Those who are telling pretend to forget the later sequences. They are thirty thousand warriors.

V

Nothing is heard. The hours pass. The warriors wait. They wait for the signal, for the crying of every day, at the same hour, and with the same rhythm. They hear nothing. The whisperings stop. They count the days. They miscount. They get it right. They laugh. They wait. One of the warriors tries his luck at climbing the enclosure, which is several yards high. He goes up the logs, hesitates, slides down, goes up again, reaches the pointed tips, peeps over, stays a few minutes. The others wait. They are impatient. The warrior comes down. His eyes pop out of their sockets. He shivers.

"He's lost his speech," says someone. The sentence crawls from mouth to mouth. It is wrapped in saliva, it receives grafts, it grows, it takes on new dimensions, and it arrives at Maguiguane's ears:

"Maddened by hunger, the men devour the women and the women devour the children. The king and the nobles point at the flesh for their banquet. No one speaks in the nkocolene."

Maguiguane laughs. The thirty thousand warriors laugh. Macanhangana sleeps. And the sentence returns to the beginning.

"Is that true?"

"We don't know. This man lost his speech. Do you want to try to climb up?"

"No. I still want to tell this to my children."

"And you?"

"No."

"Why?"

"This is not war, brother."

"You're right."

VI

The spear cuts through the air. It penetrates the mud wall. It shakes. A sound rises and is lost in the air. A crack furrows the wall, thin, shaking, sinuous. A second spear penetrates the wall a few inches higher.

The crack spreads, covers the wall from top to bottom, and small splinters fall, loose, lost. Binguane looks at the crack and no image comes to his mind. Xipenanyane sees the fracture and nothing occurs to him. A third spear is thrown. The sound hangs in the air for seconds and bigger splinters leap off, tearfully.

"If Maparato doesn't come tomorrow, we will attack," says Binguane.

"We should have done that long ago."

"They are more than twenty thousand. And we are no more than five thousand, Xipenanyane. That's why we are waiting for Maparato."

"And how many of us have already died?"

"A few."

"A few? We are already dead, all of us, father. That's why I keep asking myself: What kind of war is this?"

"Ask Maguiguane."

"I will never speak with that Nguni vassal."

"Nor he with you, Xipenanyane. But let's leave that. We have to bring the warriors together."

They separate. All along the fortification, warriors can be seen voraciously eating the shields of skin that had protected them in endless battles. Unburied dead bodies lie on the surface of the earth dug up in search of nonexistent roots. Children with enormous potbellies hunt green flies that flit over the dead bodies. Women with children cradled in their arms wander like sleepwalkers with no destination around the enclosure. Xipenanyane comes close to the northern edge of the enclosure. He sees warriors fighting over the fresh dung of the last head of cattle slaughtered for the chiefs. Three warriors fight over the intestinal liquids. A little farther away from the scene, a woman gives her urine to a child. The bushes that once used to fill the enclosure have disappeared. The houses have aged. The old people, unable to support themselves with walking sticks, crawled through the fortification on hands and knees. The children, convinced of the existence of mice, spent the afternoons making mousetraps they would destroy the following morning. And nobody cried anymore. Everybody was laughing. A laugh that stopped on their lips.

Xipenanyane lifts his hands to his face and enters a hut. On the other side of the fortification, loud guffaws rise.

VII

The warriors jump on the plain. Maguiguane makes rounds by the light of day. The spears recover the brilliance of life. The shields are rid of the mice. The days become days again. Laughter is renewed. The drums thunder. The wind is different. The trees are different. The earth is different. The blood is different. The war of all the centuries approaches. The king, miles away, wakes up in a good mood and asks about the war. Maguiguane is satisfied. Macanhangana feels that his hands are not shaking. The warriors practice. The spears whistle. The shields clash.

"We attack tomorrow, Macanhangana."

"They must be dead already."

"Future generations will rejoice with our military deeds."

Binguane feels that the words don't reach his mouth. The warriors wait. Xipenanyane advances. He already feels like a king. The warriors listen to him. They forget Binguane, the old king. They follow the words of Xipenanyane. They feel strength in their legs. They hold their spears in their hands. They stand firm.

"We are going to fight and die if necessary, but our contempt for the Nguni will remain for centuries, because this land is and will be ours. And if we fight today, it is so that our children's ears are not slashed by the Nguni. We say 'No' so that our women are not enslaved and our children do not swell the legions of that barbarian army. Justice swings to our side, warriors.

"We will go to the fight with the certainty of victory, despite this criminal siege they mounted against us, a siege that goes against the most elementary principles of war among men, cultivated by our most remote ancestors with the certainty that men face each other and that spears clash under the attentive gaze of the warriors. They started this war of snakes thinking we would die immediately. But we are alive, and our fight will be between equals, despite the high number of warriors who are outside this enclosure.

"Prepare yourselves for victory, warriors, prepare yourselves to kill these Nguni invaders. Justice is on our side and the spirits protect us.

"A while ago, I was saying to Macanhangana that the lion roars in the jungle. With that I wanted to say that the time has arrived, warriors, to go into action. For days our only objective was to give the Chope the opportunity to come to us and hand over their spears, assegais, and shields. They didn't do this. And for a simple reason: they are animals. That is what we forget, warriors. An animal used to the jungle will never live together with men and much less follow the most elementary rules of human existence. And I did not invent this truth, but it was spoken by our king, Ngungunhane, many, many years ago. At that time he invited the Chope into this big community of men that we are and that we built. They refused our generous hand and preferred to hide in the wilderness, disturbing us at night with their howls and ruining our fields. There were times when we even built kraals for these Chope animals, but they preferred the jungle and their aimless days.

"Our patience has limits, warriors. Today is the last day that we give to Binguane to surrender. Tomorrow, if he doesn't surrender with his men, we will walk over the dead bodies of those animals and will invite our king, that immortal Nguni hero, to contemplate the plain covered with dead bodies on which the birds will feast for countless centuries.

"Don't think there will be war. No, there will be no war. We don't fight like animals. We do not kill like animals. If I order you to practice, it is to chase off the laziness that you've cultivated in these days of rest. So prepare yourselves, warriors, not for the war but to kill these wild animals that call themselves Chope."

VIII

"Flames. Blood. Screams. Cries. Death. Flight . . ."

"Dead bodies . . ."

"The loneliness above all else. The silence after the bloodshed. The senseless world that remains. The emptiness that hovers after the crime."

"Death is not with the dead."

"Death stays with the brave warriors of Maguiguane."

IX

The bloodshed was of such magnitude that future generations felt the smell of the hot blood mixed with the grass. The populations of the area emigrated forever, incapable of bearing the smell of the dead, which had clung to the mud walls of the huts. The families that resisted the exodus for months saw themselves forced to abandon the area because of the simple fact that the maize tasted of human blood and water from the wells contained remains of human skeletons.

The battle lasted for one morning and one afternoon. As the night was falling, the bloodshed ended. Xipenanyane and Maparato fled with a few warriors, leaving behind the bodies of Binguane and other warriors of the Chope court. Because of the large number of dead bodies, Maguiguane ordered his men to break camp. Once they left the area, Maguiguane ordered the warriors to beat the drums of victory. But nobody, including Maguiguane, felt relieved of the tension, of the loneliness.

X

"Ngungunhane rejoiced."

"No, I don't think so. The only gesture he made was to thank the warriors for the heroic battle, and he returned to his hut without contemplating the head of his enemy."

The warriors dispersed in silence. Macanhangana returned to drinking during the nights. Maguiguane had to call a witch doctor to remove the smell of the dead from his body. And it is said that the men who came to walk over the plain of Chirrime had to walk over rotten and rotting bodies for one morning, one afternoon, and one night. Over the dead bodies lay the bodies of birds that had died because of the excesses of their feast.

Fragments from the End (5)

I congratulate Your Excellency in the name of the Portuguese government for the brilliant feat of arms that you have just accomplished, and I receive from your hands the former kinglet of Gaza, Mundungaz, known as Gungunhana; Godide and Molungo, son and uncle of the same Gungunhana, as well as his wives Namatuco, Fussi, Patihina, Muzamussi, Maxaxa, Hesipe, and Dabondi; the former kinglet of Zichacha, Matibejana, and his wives Pambane, Oxóca, and Debeza; all traitors of the Fatherland who dared to raise arms against it. I request that Your Excellency, as the governor of the district, order the issue of two notices, one stating the act of this delivery and the other acknowledging the identity of the above-mentioned prisoners.

Words of Counsellor Correia, acting governor of Mozambique, on receiving the prisoners of war from the hands of Mouzinho de Albuquerque, military governor of Gaza, on January 6, 1896.

MANUA'S DIARY

For Elias Cossa

I

Among the ruins of what used to be the last capital of the empire of Gaza, a diary was found, written in a shaky, imprecise, timid hand. The pages, in a random heap, were inside a skull lying among the skeletons of humans and animals. There is no reference to the diary's author, but it is known that it belonged to Manua, son of Ngungunhane, who at the end of July 1892 embarked on the steamship Pungué from the Island of Mozambique to Lourenço Marques. The records of the time say that the steamship left early in the morning. Full sails pulled small boats toward the coast. Dark clouds were covering the sky. Two young men waved farewell with their hats to a friend, who was disappearing on the ship. A drizzle accompanied the boat to the high sea, beyond the horizon of visibility, not much more than a few miles from the coast, where the turquoise and turbulent sea raised waves breaking on pre-Cambrian rocks, deprived of their cliffs, which had witnessed such diverse scenes as that of a one-eyed traveler named Camões, who reached these lands with a voluminous manuscript in his hands and who wrote more verses here, singing of this island while he quenched the thirst and appeased the hunger that tormented him, to the commiseration of black Muslim women who were surprised to see a filthy white and who had no idea that that thin and famished man would make known to the world a land so small that people with hobbled feet could walk across it in a week, with no effort other than looking at the scenery.

On the first night, contrary to the centuries-old custom of the Nguni, Manua ate fish. He found it tasty and cursed his people. He drank a jug of wine, burped, and left the table. He strolled through the bridge, greeted the ship's captain, and leaned against the railing, smoking a cigarette and looking at the stars and the moon, which threw threads of light on the silver mat the ship was crossing. The murmur of the waters comforted his spirit. He retired to the bunk that was reserved for him, and slept. He dreamed of spears and dry and verdant savannahs. He saw snakes winding around the fat body of his father, and smiled. At the end of the dawn, he woke up suddenly. Insistent and ferocious knocks fell on the door of his cabin. He pulled the sheets over to the left, jumped out of bed, and as he reached the door, he felt something slimy and slippery sticking to the soles of his feet. A sludge of rice covered the floor. Heads of fish with brilliant and shining eyes lay on the surface of the rice sludge. Here and there, the wine was coloring the rice, which was being soured by a yellow liquid. Enormous bubbles popped every second. It was his vomit. For a time he stood, incredulous, observing the vomit. His hands slid down the door. His body began to fold over. His knees fell to the floor. He was crying. The smell began to invade his nostrils. He put his right hand to his nose. They began to knock on the door again. With the aid of his hands, he raised himself and opened the door. The ship's captain and his two lieutenants were looking at him with some gravity.

"You're lucky that you're the king's son, boy," said the captain. "Otherwise you would clean all this shit, and then I would throw you overboard, you nigger . . . Look at this mess . . . See, look at the shit you made . . ."

A trickle that was growing until it filled the whole corridor was coming out of the cabin. It was the vomit. The vomit in shades of red and yellow. It was the fish heads. It was the smell. It was the flies buzzing. Incredible, thought Manua. He felt his legs shake and his armpits sweat as he leaned on the hallway wall. His mouth was dry and his eyes, like those of the fish, were popping out of their sockets, enormous.

"Follow me," said the ship's captain.

Everywhere the vomit was covering the floor, red, yellow. Of the fish, all that could be seen were the enormous heads. The flies were all over the hallways, entering the cabins, covering the bridge, and buzzing. The passengers leaned on the ship's railing, vomiting, unable to bear that slimy, muddy, dirty, and stinking floor. The sea around the boat was taking on the color of the vomit. Dead fish were coming to the surface. Women were screaming hysterically. Children were fainting. Men were shouting, swearing, evoking fathers and grandfathers. The cleaners were running from one end of the ship to the other with cloths and water, not knowing where to start.

And Manua was crying. Minutes later, he went back to his bunk. He lifted the sheets and saw that they were spotless except for a blot of sperm. He looked at his clothes and saw they had no stains, except for the area at his knees. He sat on the edge of the bed. The cleaners came into the cabin and wiped the floor, looking out of the corners of their eyes at the nigger, son of the king the Portuguese feared so much. They left. Manua opened his suitcase, took out paper, a pen and ink. He wrote. He spoke of his father and called him ignorant and a sorcerer. He spoke of his time as a student, stating that he once dirtied his room with shit during the night, leaving the bed clean. Today, he wrote at one point, I vomited. The ship's captain understands nothing of witchcraft. If he knew something, maybe he could understand that I have been one of the few in my tribe who had access to the world of the white people, to their language, their habits, and their science. But he cannot understand the black world, our barbarian habits, the envy that rules our lives, and the intrigues that kill us every day.

When I am emperor, I will abolish these practices, which are opposed to the Lord, father of the heavens and the earth. I will be among the first in these African lands to accept and adopt the noble habits of the white people, men I have held in high esteem since the first day I had access to their wholesome civilization.

His hand shook. He couldn't continue. He folded the paper in four, put it in his suitcase, and threw himself on the bed, trying to sleep. When night fell, the sound of the brushes over the wooden floor could still be heard. He didn't want to eat. He waited for the passengers to return to their cabins so that he could come out.

"You allow niggers on these ships and this is the result, captain. Do you know that my wife fainted?"

"No. But you, sir, must understand that the young man is the son of the king of the southern lands."

"What king, what shit, the niggers never had kings, captain! That's a myth. If I were in your shoes, I would throw him overboard. That's what he needs, fucking nigger."

"You're right, sir," said a third man, coming closer. "The captain should throw him into the sea."

"That I won't do. But it's hard for me to believe that the boy filled the ship with vomit."

"Hey, captain, be careful what you're saying! Do you think a white man like me and others around here don't know where to vomit?"

"That's not what I meant, but I find the fact hard to believe."

"This is witchcraft," said the first man who spoke to the captain. "I've been traveling all this time in the bush and I saw incredible things, captain. If I told you that I saw villages growing old from day to night, would you believe me?"

"Tell us the story, then," requested the captain.

"I'll tell you, yes, I'll tell you, and don't think that whoever tells a story embroiders on it. What I'm about to tell you is as true as Maria das Dores being the name of my wife, who suffered so much with the vomit of this damn nigger. The story took place not so long ago, it was a very short time ago; and my presence on this boat, which is taking me and my wife to Lourenço Marques, is proof of that. Me and some other Portuguese were hunting slave traders, this abominable trade done by niggers, when we learned from a black informer that we were a day's march from a village with slaves just about to embark for Madagascar. We walked for the morning, the afternoon, and part of the night through the bush, exposed to all manner of dangers, when already deep in the night we heard shrill voices. We were a few steps from the village. There was a fire in the opening. The niggers were dancing. The women, naked, twisted like snakes to the sound of the drums that would deafen any of us Portuguese, if we weren't used to traveling in these lands. They were so drunk that they were doing the shameful stuff meant for the bed in the plain light of the moon. Our mistake was to not attack them that night. We chose to surround the village and wait for daylight. And that's what we did. At the break of day, we entered the village with guns at the ready and we found it deserted. And to our surprise there were termites all over the place, and the huts collapsed at the slightest touch. In the trees all you could see were monkeys. Unbelievable. We beat the informer. The nigger, writhing in pain, confirmed that what we had just seen was witchcraft because the men, according to him, were in the trees, transformed into monkeys, and the women were the termite mounds that rose throughout the village. We didn't believe it. We left the village, and all morning the monkeys followed us in the distance. In mid-morning, we had lunch under the trees, and it crossed my mind to go back to the village. The guide came along. We arrived at the village at nightfall. The houses were like new, and the niggers were dancing and drinking."

"Unbelievable," said the captain.

The man stared with his eyes open wide.

"That's it. If I'm lying, may my father lose his balls. I saw it with these eyes. And you know what I did? I left my uniform on the commandant's desk, and I embarked on this ship with my wife. I'm going to open a store in Lourenço Marques. And if I don't return to Europe, it's because I'm broke, captain. I still have to live for many years among these niggers. And there are many more stories than that. And on second thought, captain, the best thing to do is put two men at the door of the boy's cabin. What the kid did was to show to the whites the power of nigger witchcraft."

"You are right, Mr. . . . ?"

"António Matos."

"Right, Mr. António Matos. You have to have the stomach of a whale to vomit like this. I will put two men at the door of his cabin and not let him come out, not even to the bathroom. Fucking nigger."

"It's the best thing you can do, captain. There are people here prepared to slash him to pieces. I've already seen a nigger being stabbed. Instead of blood, captain, water was coming out."

"What a race!"

"If I were the king, I would take the Portuguese from these lands and leave the niggers to their savage life, because it's useless us being here with tales of civilization. These niggers play around with us, captain. You say that the boy was studying. But I bet you that as soon as he arrives in his land, he'll take off his pants and shoes and wear his animal-skin skirts again."

"These niggers are difficult to wear down."

"It's true."

"It's getting late for me. My wife must be worried, poor thing. Good night."

"Good night."

They went their separate ways. Manua took his ear from the door and cried. The ship rolled to the right and returned to its initial position. The steps echoed ever more faintly in the ship's hallways. The captain went to the bridge. Manua threw himself on the bed.

The diary makes no mention of the following days, but it is known from other sources that the boy did not leave the cabin. The two guards tried to convince everybody that they saw strange lights moving all over the ship. But nobody believed them. On the second day of August, the steamship moored in the harbor of Lourenço Marques. The suitcases left the cabins. The passengers began to disembark. Manua was one of the last to disembark. Two warriors were waiting for him. They were carrying spears and shields. The sun was in the middle of the sky. There were layers of dust in the air. The whites, in groups of two, three, and four, were waiting to see Manua. Some were frightened by the stories that the passengers told them because not a few said that the boy, besides vomiting, brought the wind into the cabins, making the clothes fly and disturbing the people. But when you left the cabin, the wind was calm and disturbed nobody. And the worst, man, was the time when we woke up suddenly with fish coming between the sheets. They were fish this size, huge. And why didn't you catch them, mate? We sure did, but each time one went overboard, five more appeared. What witchcraft . . . And didn't you eat them? Don't say that, man, they had feet. What? Legs, man. They looked like lizards. You ought to burn the boy, brother. All you had to do was pick him up and throw him in the oven. That wouldn't work. Maybe, but if you threw him overboard, as my grandfather used to say, when the beast dies the poison ends. Don't call us stupid, mate. The captain had armed guys at the nigger's door. You are all just cowards. Not at all. See that man over there, he traveled in the bush and told us that it was useless to kill the boy, because he once saw a nigger being stabbed and instead of blood he saw hooch flowing, and a good one, brother. Booze? Brandy, man. Real witchcraft! Around here things happen, but not as bad, no. Look, there comes the boy. He dresses like a white man, mate. True, the kid doesn't look like a bum. And he has studied much more than you. Don't say that, brother, I know how to write. But the boy graduated in arts and crafts. Such a course is useless in the hands of a nigger. You're probably right, but the boy speaks good Portuguese. Oh, Portuguese and what not . . . Look, the boy has the eyes of a drunkard. It's from all the booze he drank. The captain said that the boy downed a barrel of wine. And it must be true, because vomit like that was enough to make a whale sick, brother. Wine is big business here. It's that race, they drink like dogs. But the boy is embarrassed; it's because of the witchcraft, mate. You're right. And look at those niggers waiting for him. It's their army, man. And where is he going to stay? Not at my inn for sure, I'm fed up with witchcraft. He could be going to the Albasinis. Who are they? A bunch of mulattoes. They'll get along with each other. Let's go, it's getting late, brother; the wife has a roast in the oven.

11

From 1892 to 1895, the year of Manua's death, the diary says nothing because the pages were eaten by mice. The letters that remain are dispersed. The five remaining letters put together spell the word *morte,* death. Or *temor,* fear. Or *tremo,* I tremble.

Kamal Samade, who passed through the capital, left his impressions in Arabic, written on disordered pages. From his pen we know that Manua, after his arrival, became taciturn and more of a drunkard than ever. It was normal to see him smoking mbhangui. His shoes had no soles, and his clothes had lost their initial color. He walked in his sleep, concluded Kamal Samade.

Buinsanto, who sought refuge in the Transvaal after the fall of the empire, stated that his brother Manua was drinking insatiably because of the spell cast by his great-grandparents, who became irritated when he adopted those foreign manners of walking, dressing, and speaking. His penis shrank day by day. On the day of his death, he woke up with nothing between his thighs and indulged in his biggest drinking spree ever.

Manhune told his son and grandson that Manua had been poisoned by his father because it was an embarrassment to the Nguni to see a native son assimilating the habits of other foreign peoples. And the worst thing was, Manhune used to say, that Manua behaved like a Chope because he was subservient to the Portuguese. Kill him at the next opportunity, said Ngungunhane in one of the meetings he had with the elite of the kingdom.

Sonie, who had been Ngungunhane's inkosikazi, said after her husband's deportation that Manua was already crazy when he entered the capital of the kingdom, Mangoanhana. He spoke constantly to himself in the language of the whites. He walked like a madman through the streets of the capital, insulting everybody. In the first days, we still tolerated the boy because we thought that this was what the whites did when they were studying. But soon we saw that it was not the case, because Manua began to change the order of the day, sleeping in the afternoon, changing the night to morning and the morning to afternoon. It was sad. Ngungunhane's witch doctor told everybody that the boy had eaten fish, a thing nobody believed despite Manua speaking constantly of fish.

III

On the day of his death, which happened in March of 1895, Manua woke up at five in the morning. The morning mist covered Mangoanhana. Intermittent coughing of the old people was heard. There were fires behind the huts. The dogs barked, starving. The warriors wandered around the capital in search of locusts. Women with pitchers on their hips were fetching water. Ngungunhane was sleeping.

Manua, his eyes still heavy with sleep, emerged from the low door of his hut. He saw the outlines of the trees. He saw the women's hips rubbing against the pitchers. He inhaled the morning air and stretched. He was thin and dirty. His eyes were red.

"Don't tell me you spent the night counting the sticks of the ceiling, Manua?" asked Iomadamo, Manua's brother.

"No, I slept well," he retorted.

"You've got red eyes."

"They've always been red."

"The tortoise walks with his house, Manua."

"Mind your own business, Iomadamo . . ."

His brother looked at him and said nothing. The morning mist disappeared. The sun was rising. Manua, feeling the humidity of the ground rubbing the soles of his feet, went to the kraals, which were situated south of the capital of the empire. The few cattle left were grazing in the surroundings. The warriors were bringing the locusts in small baskets. The women were coming with jugs of water on their heads. There was gambling in the huts. He smoked mbhangui. He saw stars coming down from the sky. He saw waters covering the empire and Ngungunhane floating on the water, unable to swim. The king's eyes were growing in size. His body was swelling rapidly. It blew up. Intestines and bits of flesh were drifting on the red, blue, and black waters. The water began to subside. Manua was laughing. He guffawed deeply. He slept. The warriors watched him, shook their heads, and disappeared into the huts of their camp. Ngungunhane woke up. Sonie was taking a bath. Godide was practicing with a spear. Iomadamo was drinking. Magniguane was far away from the capital. The morning advanced. The children were playing. The empire was groaning. The Portuguese were waiting. The warriors were eating locusts. The king was eating beef. The women were having more children. The children were crying. The oxen were lowing. The flies were buzzing. The lizards were approaching the clearings. The fire was burning the tree trunks. The smoke dispersed in the air. Manua woke up. He wrote his name in the sand and returned to his hut. They brought him five gallons of sope, the name given to the liquor made in these Tsonga lands. He drank. The morning passed. The afternoon arrived. The women were laughing. Ngungunhane was sleeping with Sonie. Godide was walking. Iomadamo was speaking. Buinsanto was looking at the thin cattle. The warriors were practicing. The spears rose in the air. The shields were sticking to the bodies. The sun was setting. Manua was drinking. Godide returned home. Iomadamo was chatting with the witch doctor. Buinsanto was talking with the cattle herders. Manua was screaming. Ngungunhane woke up. Sonie got dressed. The warriors were jumping and singing. Manua saw mice coming into the hut. They surrounded him. They climbed up his body. They gnawed on his shirt, his pants, his shoes, his papers, the ceiling. He tried to get out. He saw snakes at the door. He retreated. He closed his eyes. He felt his hair being devoured. He tried to kill them. They grew in number. They were filling the house. The night was coming. Manua was screaming. Nobody came to help him. He is mad, they said. An owl hooted. Ngungunhane was sleeping. Sonie was dreaming about capulanas. Godide could see the empire at his feet. Cuiu saw in a dream his nephew Ngungunhane slithering like a snake at the feet of the Portuguese. Manua was panting. The moon was rising. The owl hooted again. The dogs barked. The sope jug fell over. The liquid spread over the floor. The mice got wet. Some got drunk. The door fell down. Manua died. The owl hooted. The dogs barked. The mice were gnawing at Manua's body. The night passed. The morning broke. The women went to fetch water. The warriors went hunting for locusts. Ngungunhane was sleeping. They woke him up. Your son died, they told him. Who? he asked. Manua. Bury him, he responded and slept. The morning grew. The locusts disappeared. The clouds fled from the sky. The empire was groaning.

FRAGMENTS FROM THE END (6)

A mingi bonanga e mizeni yenu ngi ya hamba,
manje mizokusebendza ni bafazi benu . . .

You never saw me in your houses, and it is true that I am leaving,
but now you shall be enslaved along with your wives . . .

Ngungunhane's last words before his departure

NGUNGUNHANE'S LAST SPEECH

For Teresa Manjate

People will rise against people and kingdom against kingdom, and there will be hunger, plagues, and earthquakes in several places. All of this will be but the beginning of the pain.

Matthew 24

He turned suddenly to the crowd that was booing him, a few steps from the steamship that would take him into exile, and he screamed like never before, silencing the birds and the gentle breeze, and turning the men and women to stone with his cascading words that would flow, from other mouths, across many generations in nights of vigilance and insomnia because of the premonitory power they possessed that morning, with its unexceptional combination of the waveless sea, the moored steamboat, the sun with the usual color, everyday clouds, the assembled crowd, Ngungunhane speaking, his fat body swaying to the right and to the left as his eyes shone and his hands trembled to the rhythm of the words that were swelling by the minute, such as when Ngungunhane was saying to everybody, you can laugh, men, you can vilify me, but know that the night will fall again over this accursed land that had moments of happiness only with the arrival of the Nguni, who lifted you from the unfathomable depths of blindness and debauchery. It was we who raised you, men, from the night that hindered your entrance to the world of light and happiness. Our spears removed the long-hardened cataracts from your eyes, and our shields chased off the centuries-old diseases lodged in your rotting bodies. And today, you murderous and cowardly scum, you dare to taunt me with all the strength of your ragged lungs. It is the payment, I know, for the good done by the Nguni. But you know, you dogs, that the wind will bring the stench of our crimes from the depths of the centuries, and you shall live your short lives trying to dispel the wretched images of the evils of your fathers, grandfathers, fathers of your grandfathers, and other people of your ilk. You shall begin to hate your neighbors, rebuking them for the afflictions you all will suffer in your ageless huts. The hate will spread from family to family, affecting your beloved animals that will have to fight for their grazing, if they be cattle or sheep. The roosters will not go after the neighbor's hens, and the mice will divide themselves among the houses and will gnaw the possessions of only one family through countless generations. And then, you dogs, you shall not have courage to raise your heads. The hunchback will be so heavy that you shall have children and grandchildren with an interminable and hereditary hump!

"There are details that time is reducing to dust," said the old man, coughing. He put two logs on the fire and blew on it. Woolly balls of smoke passed over his face. Little tears came out of his tired eyes and grazed his skin covered with scales. I put the papers away. I looked at him. It was night.

"I was still a child," he continued, "when my grandfather used to tell me stories of Ngungunhane. And I used to be afraid. A fear I cannot explain today. But fear it was. When I slept, I always dreamed about spears and shields clashing against each other on the plain, a plain without warriors but with shields and spears that were moving, clashing constantly. I never told my grandfather about my dreams. I was afraid he would stop telling me the stories of Ngungunhane. And when he was telling them, his voice was shaking and his gestures followed the rhythm of his voice. He died in his sleep, dreaming aloud. In the morning, when I entered his hut, I saw him lying flat on his back, looking at the ceiling. He was speaking. His voice touched me deeply. For hour after hour, I listened to him talk. I wanted to wake him up because it was getting late. When I touched him, I noticed that his body was cold. He had died long ago. They had to bury him right away so that the neighbors wouldn't call us witches. And we were amazed to hear his voice coming from the hole, as if emanating from a deep chasm. My father had to sit on the grave and move his mouth to accompany the voice of the deceased. The neighbors and our other, distant relatives felt sorry for my father because they thought he was mad. Night and day, for a week and a half, my father kept opening and closing his mouth."

"What was his name?"

"My grandfather's?"

"Yes."

"Somapunga. And when he told me the stories of Ngungunhane, he dwelled on some parts that my father used to forget and that you omitted. And they are important details."

"I don't remember omitting anything."

"When Ngungunhane was speaking to the crowd that was booing him, a woman who didn't appear to be pregnant gave birth to a child without eyes and genitals. Two men suffered a heart attack."

"And nobody noticed?"

"Petrified as they were by Ngungunhane's words, I think those who saw them were few."

"Didn't the woman scream?"

"No. She must have opened her eyes and mouth before fainting. When they noticed her, she was already dead. And what impressed the people was the blood flowing in the direction of the fortress. The blood was as black as our skin. And as it advanced, it was creating a small furrow on the uphill slope. The Portuguese covered it with gravel."

"Interesting."

"Yes, it is interesting," said the old man, blowing on the fire. Little sparks jumped and disappeared into the night.

These men the color of a skinned goat whom you applaud today shall enter your villages with the noise of their guns and a whip the size of a python. They will call each of you in turn, registering you in the papers that drove Manua mad and that will imprison you. The names that came from your forgotten ancestors will die forever because you will be given names as they see fit; they will call you shit and you shall be thankful. They shall demand papers of you, even on the toilet, as if your word is not sufficient, the word that comes from our ancestors, the word that imposed order on these disordered lands, the word that brought forth children from the wombs of your mothers and wives. The scribbled paper shall guide your life and your death, children of darkness.

The women, whom you hold in such high esteem, will be fornicated with like animals in your houses or behind the houses of these animals whom today you respect more than your Nguni brothers. The women's screams of pain and pleasure will follow you everywhere, and you shall pass night after night counting the sticks of the ceiling, unable to take revenge for the infamy that afflicted the women. Many among you shall hang yourselves from dwarf trees or shall surrender to the crocodiles, which will reject you because of the cowardice you carry;

and your corpses will drift on the waters for years and years, and no water animal will come close to your rotten flesh. Others will cope with the pain and the ignominy and will begin to accompany their wives to the house of the white man, staying in the darkness of the veranda while the woman goes through the door and into the room she will leave insulted by the white man, who will force her to wash herself before getting between the sheets soiled with sperm and mud, as if she hadn't already bathed in the morning and in the afternoon, in the river or at home. The husband will bear these insults, hearing the water flow over her clean black skin while he waits, staring like a corpse, for the manic spasms of the white man and the heavy breathing of the woman who will writhe on the bed, releasing sounds from the end of times that will burst the eardrums and the veins, from which the blood and the tears of shame will flow, with the shame reaching a climax in the deepest hours of the night, when the white man, leaning from the windowsill, will throw the coin of hunger, which the husband will search for like a sleepwalker in the night without stars. He will return home in silence, incapable of speaking to his wife, who will follow stumbling over stones, ashamed, degraded.

And everywhere, like a sickness that attacks everybody, children will begin to be born with skin the color of the piss you release with pleasure in the mornings. They will be children of infamy. And for the first time in your lives you shall see children reject their mothers, who will throw themselves into houses where their bodies will be sold for the price of bread, fornicating with the offspring they won't know and pointing at random at likely fathers of the herd of children born by the dozen. Sicknesses never before seen will affect you all, and you shall not listen to the witch doctor because there will be houses where they will stick irons in your body; and there will be men dressed in women's robes who will roam fields and villages, forcing you to confess sins committed and not committed, convincing you that the spirits do nothing because everything that exists on earth and in the heavens is under the command of a being whom nobody knows but who follows your steps and your words and your actions. The night will have fallen for good on these lands whose image your sweat will transform.

You will open roads, you will ruin your feet and hands, you will drink the blood of your weakened brothers, and you shall see your women giving birth to stones and logs on the open road, and you will not be able to lift a finger because the whip they will manufacture by the minute will rip into your backs covered with fossilized ridges. You shall begin to abandon your villages, facing the shame and impotence of seeing your daughters raped in open air, your fathers killed like beasts for the slaughter, your brothers whipped for farting with fear in front of the white man who will vilify you forever and ever, burning your houses, taking over the lands that came from your ancestors, collecting taxes for the huts you built with your sweat, forcing you to work on huge farms where you will drift like sleepwalkers day and night, eating pythons and monkeys, clawing the ground with fingers worn to the bone, and cleaning the shit off your boss's child.

And wherever you go, you shall find the same images, the same degradation, the same expansion. Your brothers will ask you for papers, which you will not have in order, and you will enter houses full of irons and will go mad. You will begin to roar, climbing the walls like blind lizards, and you will howl like starving hyenas throughout the night. In the morning, they will remove you naked from the cells, with chains on your feet like cattle about to be slaughtered. You shall not sleep with your wives, who will just look at you and say the usual words in the time scheduled for the visit. Months later they will tell you that your wife had a child the color of piss. You shall break down the bars and throw yourself into the night, toward home, where you shall cut your innocent wife into pieces. And you shall return to prison for life and see your sex shrink from day to day. And those unable to cope will surrender their butt or pursue imprisoned children, turning them into women, spoiling them the way you spoil your wives, scolding them the way you scold your wives. And there the world will have changed forever.

"Ngungunhane was drooling," said the old man.

"And he couldn't see anybody anymore."

"Right, he could see nobody with his shining eyes. He was at the high point of his speech. And the most striking parts were the clouds disappearing in the sky and the whites who, despite not understanding anything, had their hair raised."

Outside the bars, your grandchildren will forget the language of their ancestors, insult their fathers, be embarrassed by their barefoot mothers, and conceal their houses from their friends. Our history and our customs will be denigrated in schools under the attentive gaze of men dressed in women's robes, who will force children to speak of my death and call me criminal and cannibal. The children will laugh at this shame, which old people without an audience will try to redeem with their version that nobody will listen to.

Everywhere, sons of darkness, you shall see death stamped on the houses you will build. You will run like lizards through these lands, searching for light to warm your reptilian scales. And at night, stuffed in cramped houses, you will feel strange steps treading on the veranda and approaching the door, which for centuries will bear an impression of the shape of ears that will listen to what you will not say. Death and mourning will spread over these lands, and flies will settle on the blackness of your skin, tired of moving between the living and rotting corpses scattered in the streets. And the time will come when you will flee to the bush, where you will begin to hunt the men of your perdition, killing one here and another there. Then you will breathe the air of your existence for just a little while, because soon you will begin to hate each other and kill each other, thinking of the throne before it has been conquered. Blood will flow, you will call each other names that your own language does not have, and you will again consult the witch doctors of your salvation, who will begin to charge in the same currency as the storekeeper asks for rice. You will kill your opponent from a distance, making him float in a pool of death, where the water will take on the color of blood. You will release killer bees on your enemies, and there will be morning mist at midday. But you will begin to learn new doctrines that will reject the spirits, the witch doctors, and the medicine men. Everyone or nearly everyone will accept the new shepherd, but in the middle of the night many will go to the witch doctor and ask for the root that protects against the enemy's bullets, because they will not want to die before tasting victory; and the witch doctor will ask for the heart of the enemy, whom you will kill without pity in an ambush of moving tree trunks. Everywhere you will feel like heroes because the bullet will pass in the distance, and if it touches you, you will only need to lean against a tree, which will wither and restore your health. Others will transform themselves into snakes, enter the enemy's camp, study their steps, and register their numbers. And such will be our victorious war against the men who entered these lands without anybody's permission. Many of those men's children will stay in these lands and will learn our languages and will dance our dances and will marry our women for all to see, and will truly be our brothers because they will exorcise the centuries of evil with the witch doctors of tomorrow.

Once victory is reached, you will have a black man on the throne of these lands. You will rejoice on seeing the cloths being raised on the rainy night of our victory. But you still will not have arrived at the time of your happiness, you dogs, because the curse that embraced these lands will last for centuries and centuries. And in the illusion of your victory, you will invade houses that you had built and you will change the order of things, beginning to shit where you should eat and eat where you should shit. The disorder will be so great that houses will change color, taking on the color of death; and death will settle in your lands, which will have the length of many months of journeying. There will be endless rain that will demolish the fields and the cities. The roads will shatter, and throughout avenues and streets snakes will begin to appear with nests for all to see, and they will confuse their hissing with the disorderly whistles of the police starved for centuries, hunting for professional thieves who steal cigarettes and batteries and potatoes and the remains of food. Oxcarts will begin to replace machines that expel smoke, and you will see the streets filled with dry and fresh dung, which the men will collect in the endless nights of hunger. Eager to eat, you will make gruel out of shit, which will cause diarrhea and vomit that will fill your concrete houses and then flow out through the hallways and staircases without steps into the gardens and streets, causing a deluge of diarrhea and vomit that will drown children and old people, men and women, who will become food for gigantic mice, free to occupy the avenues and houses without owners. These will be the first days of your disgrace, which will be completed by men roaming the bush, killing fathers and mothers, longing for the time of the whip and the sleepwalking plantations. Confusion will reign for centuries, and there will be torment by fire; the pregnant bellies of innocent women will burst, forcing the fathers to eat the stillborn without a tear in their eye. The sun will change color and the clouds will withdraw from the skies for an indeterminate time, bringing the rain by surprise and the sun when the rain is expected. And hunger will arrive at the store, where the storekeepers will spend their lives swatting flies while the entire people transform the streets into stores. The prisons will multiply, and the men in command will reach the point of arresting everybody because everybody will sell and buy things at a price that nobody knows. And the streets will be deserted. And there will be chiefs without subjects. And you will have to return to the beginning of beginnings. So it is and so will be your centuries-long disgrace, men. Now have a good laugh, men, laugh!

"And he looked at them," said the old man. "He was tired. He was sweating all over his body, and his chest was full of slobber. The crowd was looking at him, petrified. The clouds had disappeared. The waves began to appear on the waters, and the steamship began to rumble. The sun was in the middle of the sky. The women began to cry. The men, still incredulous, were looking at Ngungunhane, who was calmly cleaning the slobber. He took two steps forward and stopped. In a drawling, calm, tired voice, he said: "The rain will not come to these lands before the end of two years. You will go through the bush and will eat mice, which will disappear on the first night. Then you will look for locusts, which you will not find. You will enter the waters and you will eat fish, contrary to the oath you made during our stay in these lands. The Nguni who remain will return to Zululand because they will not be able to bear your cowardice, Tsongas without spirit!"

Having said these final words, Ngungunhane turned around and walked toward the ship, accompanied by his wives and his son and other men. He walked up the steps without once turning his face. He disappeared into the ship's interior. For one hour, approximately, they waited for the ship's departure. The engines were working. The surrounding waters were agitated. The ship was not departing. After that time, they heard a song rising in the air and the birds invading the sky. Ngungunhane was singing and dancing. His baritone voice brought tears to the eyes of the old and young who were watching the ship part the waters as it pulled away from the coast. After the boat was lost in the sea, the song covering the sky and the earth could still be heard. Ngungunhane disappeared.

He put two logs on the fire and blew on it.

"The drought invaded these lands," he continued. "The harvest was poor. Maguiguane tried to take advantage of the discontent to revolt, but the Portuguese had more strength. The empire collapsed forever and ever. It had already collapsed with the departure of Ngungunhane."

"That's it," repeated the old man. "It had already collapsed. The Portuguese won."

"But they lost in the bigger arena."

"Ngungunhane had predicted it."

"You're right. Aren't you going to sleep?"

"I'm going to sleep here, next to the fire."

I stood up. I was tired. The clear, cloudless night was giving complete freedom to the moon. I began to move away from the fire. With his head resting between his hands, the old man was sobbing. I began to walk faster. I don't know why, but as I was listening to the old man's crying, I was speeding up my step. I moved away from the hut that was reserved for me and turned my face toward the fire. Between two huge mango trees, the old man, with his head between his hands, was not seeing the fire and the night. He was crying. And I was moving away from the hut, from my room, and throwing myself into the moonlit night. Something intrigued me about the old man and about Ngungunhane's speech.